"Maki[ng] [Love Just Doesn't Happen]
Quite So Matter-Of-Factly.

"At least not in the movies I've been to. Things happen if they're supposed to. Isn't that the way it is?"

"I don't know, Jane," Max replied. "Maybe I missed that movie."

"Maybe I missed it, too. I don't seem to have the right comebacks."

"I'll give you some. Jane's comeback number one: 'Sure, Max, what the hell. Let's do it and see what happens.'" He ran one finger along the loose neckline of her sweatshirt. "Comeback number two: 'Nope, sorry. Get lost, bub. Bad idea.'"

"Is there a third?" she asked.

"Uh-huh. An old standby. Easy to remember, and it worked for Valentino and Bogart, to name but a few." He lowered his head, then closed the small space between them and kissed her slowly and deeply.

Dear Reader:

Sensual, compelling, emotional . . . these words all describe Silhouette Desire. If this is your first Desire, let me extend an invitation for you to sit back, kick off your shoes and enjoy. If you are a regular reader, you already know what awaits you—a wonderful love story!

A Silhouette Desire can encompass many varying moods and tones. The books can be deeply moving and dramatic, or charming and lighthearted. But no matter what, each and every one is a terrific romance written by and for today's women.

I know you'll love March's *Man of the Month*, *Rule Breaker* by Barbara Boswell. I'm very pleased and excited that Barbara is making her Silhouette Books debut with this sexy, tantalizing romance.

Naturally, I think *all* the March books are outstanding. So give into Desire . . . you'll be glad that you did!

All the best,

Lucia Macro
Senior Editor

SALLY GOLDENBAUM

THE PASSIONATE ACCOUNTANT

SILHOUETTE *Desire*

Published by Silhouette Books New York

America's Publisher of Contemporary Romance

SILHOUETTE BOOKS
300 East 42nd St., New York, N.Y. 10017

ISBN: 0-373-05557-9

First Silhouette Books printing March 1990

Printed in the U.S.A.

Books by Sally Goldenbaum

Silhouette Desire

Honeymoon Hotel #423
Chantilly Lace #460
Once in Love with Jessie #520
The Passionate Accountant #557

SALLY GOLDENBAUM

Born in Wisconsin, Sally now lives in Missouri where she has been successfully writing contemporary romance novels for the past five years, as well as teaching at the high school and college level. Married for almost twenty years, Sally also holds a master's degree in philosophy and has worked both as a textbook writer and as a public relations writer for public television.

Prologue

—

This is Max Harris. Sorry to have missed your call. Please leave your name and number at the beep."

Beep. "Mr. Harris, this is Jane Barnett calling you about the information you sent my office for your tax returns. It is Friday, seven-ten a.m. I cannot begin work on your returns until we talk. Thank you."

Beep. "Ms. Barnett, Max Harris here. Sorry I missed you again. I think our hours make it impossible for us to connect. Is there a problem with the returns?"

Beep. "Mr. Harris, Jane Barnett again. Friday noon. Our schedules still seem to be at odds. I'm usually not in the office at midnight. Maybe if you called earlier..."

Beep. "This is Max. Sorry about the midnight call. My days and nights were twisted around. Now about those returns..."

Beep. "Mr. Harris, I'm afraid if we can't connect soon, the returns will not get in this year. Your last call came on a Saturday. Please try Monday through Friday."

Beep. "Max here. I'm really sorry. I think you're a little—shall I say peeved?—at me. My secretary got married and I have this job, you see..."

Beep. "You have a job, and I have a job. And mine, right now, involves weeding through a hundred scraps of paper and torn receipts that smell like celery and carrots and don't make much sense, Mr. Harris. Jigsaw puzzles are not my area of expertise. Perhaps an accountant nearer your office..."

Beep. "No, listen, I'm sorry. I can explain. It's my secretary—she got married. And the job will be over soon."

Beep. "Mr. Harris, I have waited. Far too long. Today's torn receipts showed eight hundred dollars in balloons, a carousel, a sailboat—and the truth. I've been had. I don't know why, but I hope you've enjoyed the prank. Goodbye, Mr. Harris." *Click.*

One

——

Max Harris drove slowly up and down the narrow streets in the hilly neighborhood.

It was a quiet place filled with nondescript houses on small plots of carefully tended land. Dark elms leaned over the street shading cars parked along the curb and children playing in small square front yards.

Homey, Max thought. Definitely homey. And not exactly what he had expected. Jane Barnett had talked about her office. So he had thought about an office—the shiny, glass-fronted Michigan Avenue kind. But Jane's address had led him west of downtown into a neighborhood inhabited by factory workers and small, young families.

It had disturbed Max slightly when the last message the accountant had left was angry. And final. In his profession he made enough enemies without doing it over the phone with a stranger. But hell, he couldn't really blame her for getting tired of it. If it hadn't been for that witless case that had him dressed up as a cowboy at a trade show, he'd have managed to call her at a sensible hour. Oh, well. Max Harris knew as well as anyone that you win some and lose some.

He slowed down, checked a street address, then drove on. All right, he thought, what was next? He'd made a royal mess of his records ever since Franny left to get married. Every day he stared at the long list of To Do's that read "Hire Another Franny" on the very top, but somehow the days slipped away too fast. Too much work. He needed a vacation and that was just around the corner. As a present to himself, Max had cut down considerably on his client load for the next couple of months.

Max grinned at the thought and ran his fingers through his hair. "Haircut." That was on the list, too.

A young child with long braids darted across the street. Max slammed on the brakes. The little girl darted off into the shadow of a white-shingled garage without ever giving him a backward glance. He resisted the urge to go after her and lecture her on the dangers of tempting fate, but a glance at his watch told him he better do what he was here to do—reclaim his sack of receipts from Jane Barnett, then meet Uncle Leo down at his place for a beer. And he would apologize to the accountant for the mess he'd dumped in her lap. Max didn't like to inconvenience people like that, especially one with a sexy voice that had been damned nice to come home to.

He thought again about Jane's voice. He had gotten used to hearing it, to the slight lift, the throaty laugh. It was an unusual voice, rich and velvety. It had intrigued him, although he supposed it was the mystery of the bodiless voice that piqued his imagination.

Well, no matter, he'd blown it and couldn't blame her for not wanting to wade through the scraps of paper he called his records.

Max slowed the car down to a crawl and scanned the shiny brass numbers on the doors. There it was. Eight hundred twenty. It was a small white house set at an angle on the hilly street and it was tucked in tightly among all the others in the plain neighborhood. Still, the house stood out from the rest. It sparkled. Vibrant beds of newly planted flowers provided a colorful contrast to the clean gray sides of the house, and a single giant oak tree shaded the entire front lawn.

Max parked his car, climbed the steps in three loose strides and dropped the heavy brass knocker against the plate on the green door. He was smiling. It was the house, he decided; the house made him smile.

Max waited a moment, then dropped the knocker again. He rechecked the brass numbers. Maybe he had the wrong address. Just as he was about to turn away, he heard hurried footsteps in the hallway. And then the door was pulled open by a slender woman in a tailored green dress that matched both the door and her eyes. Her golden-brown hair was pulled back so severely that at first it looked to be as short as a man's, but when she moved slightly, Max could see the prim knot at the base of her neck. Tiny wisps of hair escaped the restraint and curled softly about her face.

"Hello," she said.

Max recognized the voice right away, those wonderful rich tones. But the rest of her surprised him, although he hadn't realized until that moment that he had conjured up images of Jane Barnett in his mind. On the machine her voice was alluring and sexy when she became angry. But the woman in front of him was very carefully and tightly composed.

When she smiled small dimples appeared beside a wide mouth and her eyes sparkled with a slight hint of openness. But when the gesture of politeness disappeared, her prim facade returned.

"Hello, Ms. Barnett," Max said.

Jane hesitated at the familiar bass voice, but she couldn't place it immediately. She frowned, puzzled. "You are...?" She dropped her hand, and a cool, protective mask slipped into place over her face. "Do we have an appointment?"

"No, not really. I came to pick up—"

"You!" she exclaimed. "Of course. The balloon man."

Max held out his hand. "An apologetic one."

Jane ignored it and stared at the man who stood confidently on her small porch. A shock of dark hair fell carelessly over his wide forehead, and she watched him push it back roughly, authoritatively. There was just the tiniest fleck of gray at his temples, but it stood out against the black hair. His face was tan, unusual for spring, and he had a rough outdoor look that made Jane think of wind and oceans. It was a nice face, lean, friendly, his features slightly uneven. Not the kind of face to which she had connected the careless words on the answering machine. But Jane Barnett didn't put much stock in appearances. "Hello," she said carefully.

"I've caused you a lot of time and trouble," Max said. He could tell from her reticence that she was still peeved. "I'm sorry," he added. "Really..."

Jane bit down on her bottom lip. His voice enveloped her. It was deep and even and had none of the flippancy of his phone messages. "Well," she said at last, "I suppose I owe you an apology, too, for my abruptness on the phone. It has been a long and busy month."

"I didn't take it personally," Max said. He smiled. "But my answering machine is sure a mess."

She seemed to relax at that but the hint of a smile disappeared quickly, and Max could see she didn't smile readily, at least not with strangers. Each time she did he wanted to tell a joke and coax the expression back on to her smooth, sculpted face.

"You do keep horrible records, you know," Jane said, and Max felt as though he had just been told his room was a mess and he couldn't have anybody over to play.

He nodded. "Yeah. Keeping records is not exactly my strong suit."

"Put mildly," Jane said.

Max laughed. Hell, she might not win any Miss Congeniality awards, but beneath her studied composure he suspected there just might be a sense of humor. Maybe even some soul, although she was trying damn hard not to show it.

Jane shifted uncomfortably beneath his stare, then scolded herself. She wasn't usually cowed so easily. She had nearly perfected the art of keeping men at the right distance. But there was something about Max Harris that was affecting her, that was causing a rustling inside of her, and it made her very uncomfortable. "Why are you here?" she asked solemnly.

"Here?" Max repeated, not sure for a minute what she was asking. He was looking at her eyes. They were flecked with gold, and the tiny spots seemed to dance when the sunlight hit her face just right.

"That was a silly question," Jane said. "I guess you came for your records."

"I guess I have." Max shoved his hands into his jeans and grinned. "Unless you've had second thoughts and want to save me from the clutches of the IRS. They're not always nice people, I hear."

For a moment Jane didn't say anything. With steady green eyes she examined his face and tried to see behind the rough, handsome charm. She didn't need tax messes; she didn't need a client who couldn't be reached at home except in the middle of the night; and above all she didn't need a client whose incredible blue eyes made her lose her train of thought. But she *did* need the business and the money. Badly.

Finally she spoke. "Tell me this much, Max Harris—how did you get my name?"

Max hesitated. He wasn't sure how she would react to his answer. He was doing a friend a favor; that's why he'd sent his tax records to her. Max did lots of people favors, and he didn't hesitate to ask favors back when he needed them. When Harry Wiggins, a close friend of his Uncle Leo and teacher at the university, had suggested to Max that he give his account over to one of his former students, he had said sure. That was an easy favor as favors go. This woman was very good, Harry had said, and could use another client or two. So Max had sent his affairs to her, all bundled together with rubber bands and stuffed into a paper sack. "A friend of my uncle recommended you," Max said finally.

"Who?"

"Harry Wiggins."

Jane shook her head and allowed a small laugh to soften the lines of her face. It was that throaty laugh Max remembered distinctly from the tape on his answering machine. He could see her visibly relax as she made the connection.

"So Professor Harry is still trying to drum up business for me."

Max smiled. "Yeah, looks like it. But I do need help."

"Oh, Mr. Harris, that goes without saying!"

Max laughed at that and decided that yes, there was soul here. "Is that a 'Yes, Max, I'll save you?'" he asked.

Jane spoke slowly and deliberately. "Well, frankly, the professor is right. I can use a few new clients. Why don't you come in and we can talk about it." She stepped aside, and he walked past her into a small, cheerful entryway. "I can't promise miracles," she was saying to his back, "but we can at least give it a try. My office is to the left."

Max let her pass him and followed her down a sky-lit hallway lined with colorful paintings of lakes and mountains. There was a nice odor about the house, a mixture of plants and sunshine and fresh paint.

"Your house is very nice," he said.

"Thank you."

"Someone put in a lot of work here."

"Yes," Jane said. Her house meant a great deal to her; it had taken hard work, great sacrifice and nearly all her money, but it had been worth it. She had needed a home badly and she had managed to create one.

"It looks like an old row house that found the fountain of youth."

"Yes. I had a friend at the university who was studying design," Jane said, offering the personal information reluctantly. "He helped me. He considered it the ultimate challenge, I think."

"The house?"

"And me. I had definite ideas and very little money, so it took plenty of give-and-take. But we ended up with a home. Not perfect, but it suits us."

It suits us. The words lingered uncomfortably in Max's head. Was she married? He glanced at her hand and noticed with a peculiar relief that her fingers were bare. Then he remembered what Harry Wiggins had said: divorced. For a while now, he'd added. Nasty affair. And he had used the words "brave" and "gutsy" when describing Jane Barnett. At the time the words had no relevance, but Max wondered about them now.

They had reached the door to Jane's office, and Max shoved his thoughts aside for later and walked in, knowing before he looked around that it would be tasteful and simple. It would be like Jane Barnett.

He sat down on an old straight-backed chair that had a blue seat cover on it. "So, you think I need miracles?" he asked.

"Either that or an extremely patient tax accountant. Both wouldn't hurt." Jane walked across the room with the grace of a ballet dancer and disappeared for a moment into a small closet. She reappeared almost instantly with a familiar grocery sack in her hand. An oblong piece of paper stapled to it read M. Harris in bold, black letters. She sat down behind her desk and pushed the bag to one side. She looked at it, then at Max and then she lifted one shoulder in a small gesture and said, "There's a lot of work to do here."

Max glanced at the bag and tried to concentrate on what was in it. For reasons that could only be explained by whatever was going on in his gut, it was difficult to think business with Jane Barnett just a desktop away.

"Basically," Jane continued when Max didn't answer, "we need to get some information down. I have another appointment shortly, so I really can't go into everything with you now." Her words were short, clipped and businesslike.

Max wanted to go back home and call her up on her answering machine. "Listen," he said. "I understand completely. I sent you a mess."

Jane slipped on a pair of large horn-rimmed glasses and looked from the papers to Max. Her face was serious, her eyes clear and calm. He thought he detected a hint of laughter in her voice, but since it didn't match the expression on her face, Max chalked it up to tricks of his imagination.

"Yes, you did," Jane said. "But we'll work it out."

"Good, great. I appreciate it." He leaned forward and balanced his arm on his knees.

Jane glanced at the crumpled bag. "This will have to wait until I get some basic information from you—profession, source of income, investments." She slipped off her glasses and reached for a manila envelope that was on top of a neat stack of folders on the corner of her desk.

Max was suddenly embarrassed. He hoped she didn't empty the mess out on her desk. It would be a desecration of the room's neatness.

"So," he said, his thumbs circling one another, "you need more info."

She nodded. "Simple things, like what you do for a living. Accountants need to know that."

Her voice was low and direct.

"Sorry. I had that somewhere. I guess I forgot to put it in."

"But you do work, Mr. Harris?"

"Max, please. Anyone who has looked into the intimacy of my brown paper bag can, at the very least, call me Max."

Again there was that half smile. "All right, Max," she said.

"As for the job situation, I do work, although some people would debate that. Uncle Leo, for example. He thinks it's all a grand game of cops and robbers."

"You're a policeman?" Jane looked up through her glasses in surprise. She didn't like to stereotype people, but Max Harris did not look like a policeman.

"No. I was once, but now I'm a P.I."

"Private investigator," she said aloud, as if confirming it to herself.

"Right." People reacted to that in a million different ways: excitement, curiosity, incredulity, laughter. Some women found it a turn-on, and some simply thought P.I.'s were little boys who never grew up. Jane Barnett didn't react one way or another. She kept her face calm, her eyes clear and intelligent, thoughtful.

"Oh," she said. Inside herself, Jane's stomach turned over. She wasn't sure why, but P.I.'s made her think of police, and police made her think of courts, and courts made her think of a past that she never wanted to think about again. "All right, well if you can get your W-2s together, if you have those, or an income statement, and send that over here—"

"Sure." Max tented his fingers beneath his chin and watched her shuffle the papers on her desk. He wondered what she was thinking beneath that steady look.

"Here." Jane handed him an envelope containing several forms. "This is what you need to fill out. And there's a checklist so you won't forget anything. I'm not being nosy," she said. "It just makes my job a little easier. You can fill these out at home and then we'll have to get together again."

Max said yes so quickly he wondered if she thought it peculiar. No, he decided, she probably thought he cared about his taxes. Well, maybe he was beginning to. He smiled.

Jane looked up. "I missed something?"

"No. Sorry. I think your plan is a good one." He folded the envelope in half and stuck it in the pocket of his jacket. There must be something else they hadn't covered, something that would keep him there a little longer. He liked watching her and trying to bring expression to that lovely face. He was intrigued by that careful, composed look that matched her profession, the dancing flecks in her eyes that didn't. And that wonderful head of thick burnished hair that looked so restrained he wanted to reach over and snap the band that held it, freeing it to curl about her high cheekbones.

"Well, then, I think that's it for a while," Jane said carefully. She was standing now, holding herself still beneath his scrutiny.

"Oh." Max shook his head slowly and laughed. "Sorry. I was lost in thought, I guess."

Jane nodded, her face impassive but for the tinge of color coating her cheeks.

"When you're ready for me, just give a call," Max said.

His phrasing seemed to strike them both at the same time. Jane lowered her head and straightened some more papers.

"I mean—" Max began.

Jane interrupted. "I know what you meant. But that didn't seem to work too well last time. Maybe it'd be better if we set a time right now." She opened a leather date book on her orderly desk and scanned the page. "How about next Monday at eleven?"

"A.m. or p.m.?"

Jane looked up at him, straight into the dark pool of his eyes. They were deep midnight blue, so dark they appeared almost black in the shadows of the room. But when he looked at her, the darkness was lit with gentle humor, and tiny lines fanned out from the corners. The effect was a warm river of pleasure that coursed through her body. Startled, she quickly braced her shoulders and lifted her chin a fraction of an inch, a habit she'd acquired these past few years when something frightened or threatened or surprised her. She smiled with practiced coolness. "Whichever is more convenient for you," she said.

"The morning is just fine."

Max wondered at the change in her. He was trained to see slight changes, innuendoes, and he had seen the tense, sudden, pulling back immediately. But she hadn't been successful in hiding the blush that swept across her face and the vulnerable look that lingered for a few seconds afterward. Max experienced a sudden urge to protect her from all lurking evil spirits and danger, to ease away the uncertainty that rested on the finely sculpted bones of her face. It was a crazy thought.

"Thanks for not throwing me to the wolves," he said. "I'm in your debt."

"Well, better mine than the IRS's," Jane said.

"Far better."

Jane stood, and Max knew he was being dismissed. There wasn't any reason to stay longer and Jane was busy. And standing up Uncle Leo was bound to bring lightning and thunder down in the middle of his bed. But his feet didn't seem to get the message, or maybe another part of him was simply sending different directives.

Jane looked up. "Is anything wrong?"

Max shoved his hands into his pockets and collected his thoughts. There wasn't anything wrong that he could think of. But something was happening, right here, in this sunny, orderly office. There was a stirring between him and the reserved accountant. Uncle Leo would say he had slept with his head in a pool of moonlight. Maybe that was it. It made as much sense as anything else.

"No," he said finally. "Nothing's wrong. Thanks again for your time." He reached across the desk and shook her hand, a polite, impersonal gesture that felt oddly intimate. He pulled his hand away and ran his fingers through his hair. And on the way to the car he decided Uncle Leo was wrong. To feel this way, he must have slept *on* the moon.

Jane reached in the darkness for the robe at the foot of her bed. The white digital numbers on the bedside alarm clock illuminated the darkness. Two-thirty.

She moaned out loud as she wiggled her toes into a pair of slippers. Two-thirty, a full day of work ahead of her—and she was as wide-awake as her six-year-old son Dewey after a monsterish nightmare.

Jane padded softly into the kitchen, poured herself a mug of milk and set it in the microwave. She didn't like milk, and it had been at least two dozen years since she'd had warm milk. But her mother had always claimed it would induce sleep faster than two shakes of a lamb's tail. And sleep she needed desperately.

It must be the extra work, she decided as she thrummed her fingers lightly on the slick white countertop. Her eyes flitted over Dewey's colorful drawings on the doors of the refrigerator. Yes, it was the work. Most clients waited until the last minute to bring her the papers, and then wanted their tax forms done yesterday. "The way of human nature," Professor Wiggins had stressed in a beginning accounting class. Jane had been older than most of the students and clung more tenaciously to every word the wise old man said, and she had vowed she would be so organized that people's lateness wouldn't affect her. She could handle it. And so far she'd been successful. She'd been calm and cool and efficient. Until Max Harris seduced her by means of her own answering machine.

The thought of him made her catch her breath. The crayon drawings across the room blurred into a kaleidoscope of color.

He had been nice. And there was character in his face. But there was something else there, too, and it didn't have much to do with being nice or taxes. Jane hadn't felt that kind of sexual electricity in a long time. The vibrations she had felt were as powerful as a chemical reaction between two unwitting elements.

Jane opened the microwave and took out the milk. It was hot and burned her tongue. "Damn!" she said, and set the mug down on the counter. Tears smarted at the corners of her eyes. She stared through the window into the black night. Peace. Security. That was all she'd asked for Dewey and herself. That was all she wanted. And it was all evolving just the way she'd carefully orchestrated it. It would be foolish and crazy to rock the boat.

That was why she couldn't sleep. She knew it now. It wasn't the long hours of work. It wasn't worrying about having enough money for Dewey's private school. It wasn't worrying about overdue bills. It was Max.

Max Harris was a boat-rocker.

Two

He woke up thinking about Jane Barnett. The fact disturbed him, because Max Harris prided himself on waking up each morning totally refreshed. He put the world behind him when he went to sleep, never dreamed, and woke up a new person. By the time he'd had a cup of coffee and run a few miles with his sheepdog, Potter, he was ready to tackle any client and any job.

But five days after meeting Jane Barnett, Max was still having trouble finding the morning paper. He woke up tired and although he wouldn't admit to dreaming, Jane Barnett's face was becoming more and more familiar to him. It was always there, and the damnable thing was, he couldn't figure out why; her aloofness was intriguing, but her inflexibility wasn't.

He could see, even in her austere style, that there was genuine beauty beneath her composed facade, but none of that accounted for this feeling. He tried to push her away, to banish her to the faintest fringes of his consciousness, but she refused to budge.

This morning he ran an extra mile to clear out the cobwebs. But when he finally had the coffee made and was sitting at the kitchen table with the *Chicago Tribune* in front of him, Max fell sound asleep.

The ringing of the phone woke him. His voice was muffled when he said "hello." The voice at the other end was rich and clear. "Mr. Harris, this is Jane Barnett."

He pulled his brows together and stretched the cramped muscles between his shoulders. Jane Barnett. There she was again. Now she was invading his phone calls.

"Mr. Harris?"

Jane Barnett. He forced his mind to clear. "Hello. I'm, ah, sorry. I'm a little groggy here."

"I see." Her voice dropped off for a second as if she were thinking. Then she spoke again. "Mr. Harris, it's a half hour after we were supposed to meet—"

He glanced at the clock above the stove. Damn! "I'm sorry, it seems I—"

"You don't have to explain. I'm only calling to tell you I have meetings downtown today so it would be futile for you to come this late. We'll have to reschedule."

"Where? Your meetings, I mean."

"State Street."

"Okay. If you need this stuff right away, I could meet you somewhere after your meetings—"

"Well—" Jane hesitated.

"It's up to you. But it might speed things up. I've pulled together everything you need."

"Where?"

"Pardon?" Max scratched his head. Then he grabbed for the cup of coffee. He gulped it down, and at the taste of the cold, harsh liquid, he jerked and was finally fully awake.

"Where could we meet?" Jane asked.

"Anywhere. My place? I don't live far from—"

"Maybe a restaurant. A coffee shop, family restaurant, that sort of thing—"

"Sure. Right." He thought hard. What a crackpot suggestion, *his* place. Jane Barnett wasn't the kind to do business in the intimate surroundings of some stranger's apartment. For all she knew, he could be Jack the Ripper. "There's a great place near the water. Big booths. We'd be able to talk."

"All right, fine," Jane said coolly. "Tell me how to get there and I'll meet you at five-thirty, if that's convenient."

"That'd be fine." Max gave Jane the directions and hung up. It was noon. He'd slept until noon on a cold table. He shook his head. It was a premature mid-life crisis if he'd ever seen one.

Jane slipped the strap of her leather briefcase over her shoulder and walked out into the fading sunlight. She glanced at her watch. Five-fifteen. As usual she was running right on time.

During a break in her last meeting she had wondered briefly if she had made a mistake in agreeing to meet Max Harris. For over five years now Jane had schooled herself in being objective. Having already made one nearly deadly mistake in judgment, she was determined never to repeat the error. Something lurked in the back of her mind that made her wary of Max, a tiny prickle that made her uneasy. It might have been that it was his face and not his tax forms that had come to mind when she thought of him, and she could still hear his voice, the loose laugh that made her want to smile. She had been half tempted to call and cancel the appointment, to say she couldn't handle any more clients after all.

But if she was going to succeed as a businesswoman, she had to act like one—calm, cool and collected. And the fact that he missed the appointment only meant she was the more professional one, and she'd better act like it.

A smile slipped into place, and a good-looking man passing her on State Street tipped his head and smiled back. Jane blushed.

She crossed the street at the light and turned the corner as Max had directed. Several blocks later she began scanning the row of storefronts for the coffee shop. The street was filled with renovated buildings and colorful signs, but there didn't seem to be a restaurant in sight. Looking down a small walkway between buildings, she spotted a flight of stairs and a small sign. Leo's Landing, it said. She checked the address Max had given her. It matched.

Slowly she walked down the cobblestone walk. She looked up at the building that had probably been a warehouse at one time before it was gutted and transformed. The place looked friendly and warm, but it definitely wasn't a coffee shop.

Max was at the bar when she walked in, and slid off the stool immediately. "Hi. Glad you found it."

"Hello, Mr. Harris. This is a coffee shop?" She looked around at the polished cherry tables and framed posters of Chicago landmarks and the city's famous and infamous figures. A group of nicely dressed men and women were laughing and talking at the bar.

Max looked around, not sure what she meant. Then his eyes widened. "Oh, the bar." He gave a small laugh. "Sorry. When you said family place, I thought of this..."

Jane lifted one brow.

"There's a great restaurant in the back, and Leo's my uncle." He shrugged, and one corner of his mouth lifted up slightly.

Jane shook her head. "Okay. I was thinking more of a Howard Johnson's. Different mind-sets, I guess."

Max took her by the elbow and began leading her around the brass-edged bar. "Sure, I can see that. But you'll love this place, Jane. Leo keeps it warm and friendly, and the restaurant is the best kept secret in Chicago. You have my word."

"I don't intend to eat."

"Oh, all right. We'll work then. But for future reference you need to come back and try his mushroom soup."

Jane nodded, hurrying to keep up with his long strides. Her stomach knotted. Business luncheons were one thing, but meeting with Max Harris at a place called Leo's Landing was a mistake.

They passed through the cheerful bar and entered a long carpeted room. Wide windows looked out over the river. Jane smiled her stiff professional smile and vowed to make the best of it. "Let's sit in that booth over there. We can spread things out and get this over with in a hurry."

"How much time do you have?"

The question threw her completely off balance. She had the whole evening but that was of no concern to Max. On Tuesday nights Dewey went off with Sara and George Jennings, Jane's dearest friends in the world, so she had no commitments and usually spent the night catching up on work. Jane thought George's influence, a man's influence, in her six-year-old son's life was important. But Sara's constant reminder that what Dewey really needed was a full-time father was lost on Jane. She knew far too much about full-time fathers. "I have enough time to get the work done," she said to Max. She slipped into the booth.

"Oh, okay." Max looked at her carefully across the polished cherry tabletop. He'd scared her and he didn't know why. "I've got those forms all filled out. Here." He slipped a manila envelope across the table. "Now, I think that accomplishment calls for a drink."

Jane had opened her briefcase and taken out a pad of paper. At his suggestion, she looked up, her glasses firmly in place.

A protection, Max thought. "Would you like a drink?" he asked.

"White wine would be fine." That was probably a mistake, too, Jane thought. But in the intimacy of the comfortable booth, she needed fortification and something to calm her nerves.

Max gave the order to a friendly waiter who greeted Max by name, disappeared, and was back in seconds with a scotch, a glass of wine and a platter of cheeses with slices of warm sourdough bread piled in a linen-lined basket.

Jane looked over at Max. "This really is a nice place," she said, and smiled. And Max was a nice, kind man. So why was she so uptight? She took a sip of wine and tried to calm down.

"I know," Max said. He smiled, too, glad to see her relax.

Jane set the glass back down. She scanned the sheets he had carefully filled out. "And it looks like you've given me everything I need. Now if you could just answer a few questions."

"Sure, shoot." Max settled back in the seat, slowly drank his Scotch and watched Jane Barnett. He had crammed two weeks' work into the afternoon hours and he was wiped out. But right now, sitting across from Jane like this, things were certainly tolerable.

Jane pointed to a notation on her pad with the sharpened tip of her pencil. "The balloons. You gave me a receipt for three thousand balloons."

Max nodded and helped himself to a piece of thick yellow cheese. "You're wondering why I bought them?"

"Actually, that's none of my business. But you listed it as a deductible expense, and I need to know what category it fits into."

"Oh, sure. I should have been more specific. I'm sorry."

His apology was accompanied by a warm smile, and Jane took another sip of wine.

"The balloons were for a circus," Max explained. "Usually clients cover that expense. I was working undercover in a circus to check out some theft. Anyway, I needed balloons for my stand, and the supply guy was out so I bought my own and I guess I went a little crazy. It was a circus for kids down on the South Side, and I thought it would be terrific to have huge helium balloons made up to look like animals—"

"I get the picture." Jane laughed softly. Two thousand balloons. She vowed to never, ever hire Max should she be in need of a private eye.

"The guy who hired me wouldn't cover them."

"Not very nice of him."

"Oh, well. You win some, you lose some. But it didn't matter too much because the kids loved them."

"Did you figure out the theft?"

Max laughed. "It was the gorilla trainer. He hid the bucks in the cage under Mazie the gorilla. Mazie must have liked me because one day when I was walking through the tent—I'd already figured out who did it but had no evidence—Mazie started to throw dollar bills at me. And then I swear she grinned."

Jane nibbled on a piece of bread and felt a pleasurable warmth envelope her as she listened to Max. It was the story, she guessed, or Max maybe. Or the flickering lights that were now dotting the riverfront below them. When the waiter refilled her glass, she hardly noticed.

"So," Max said across from her, "that takes care of the balloons. What's next?"

Jane focused on the list in front of her. She pushed the wine glass to the side. "Okay, next we have a trip to San Francisco."

For forty-five minutes Jane asked questions and Max dutifully answered them. And by the time Max's stomach growled for the first time, Jane was closing her briefcase.

"Jane, you can't leave me now."

Jane took off her glasses and slipped them into her purse. "I'm finished. I have to get home."

She started to rise but was stopped by a firm hand on her shoulder.

"So, my Maxie brought a friend?" said a booming voice at her elbow.

Startled, Jane turned and looked into a pair of lively brown eyes. They were a deep, chocolate brown, and a million laugh lines spread out from the corners.

"Maxie?" Jane whispered. Then, regaining her balance and her decorum, she spoke again. "Hello. I'm Jane Barnett."

"And I'm Leo, Jane. Maxie's Uncle Leo." He reached for her hand and pumped it enthusiastically. "And I'm delighted to meet you and have you here in my restaurant. Welcome! And sit," he added, convincing her by pushing gently on her shoulder.

The elderly man was about Jane's height, and his happy eyes never once left her face. He had a thinning shock of gray hair that seemed to have been combed in all different directions. "So, Jane, have you had the soup yet?"

"Sorry, Leo, you're too late," Max said. "Jane is leaving."

Leo looked at Max for the first time. "Ha, leave? Leave where?"

"Depart, leave. Go home," Max said.

Max looked at his uncle with affection and amusement. Jane had the distinct feeling the two could read each other's minds. Between the two of them she wouldn't stand a chance.

Leo drew his thick white brows together. "Jane, have you eaten dinner? I see nothing here but bread and cheese. You could use some food, fatten you up a little."

When he touched her cheek gently Jane smiled up at him. Had she been a more outgoing person, she thought she might have hugged him. "It was wonderful bread, Leo. Very, very good."

Leo was shaking his head. "It doesn't compare to the mushroom soup. No, dear Jane, you can't leave my place without tasting the soup—my own mother's recipe," he added, squeezing his fingers together and punching the air for emphasis.

"Hey, Leo, no need to build a case for the confessional here," Max said.

"Okay, so my mother couldn't cook. But my, oh my, can my chef! Wonderful, wonderful stuff. You stay, Jane, and you will never, ever regret it. You have my solemn promise." With a short, square hand he was grasping his heart now, and Jane found herself laughing along with Max.

"What can I say?" she said. The truth was she wanted to stay. But she didn't know if it was Leo's gracious insistence, or the queer pleasure she felt in Max Harris's company.

Leo had lifted her hand from the tabletop, and now he kissed her fingers lightly. "Jane, simply say you will stay to dine and you have made me a happy man. Such a simple gesture to bring such great happiness to an old man."

Max moaned. "Leo, enough already."

Leo slapped his nephew on the back. "What kind of thanks is this? I get a beautiful woman to share your table and you moan?" The gray-haired man rolled his eyes dramatically. Then he pulled himself together and glared at them both. "Enough chatter. Drink, eat, be merry, you two. I will order up a dinner for you that will surely put you in paradise."

He turned without further talk and walked slowly back across the thick carpet, chatting with other diners, asking about relatives' marriages and sick cousins. His back was stooped slightly, and he grasped the backs of chairs as he walked, but his booming voice was vibrant and won smiles from every table he passed.

Jane watched him go. "He's a very nice man. How have I gone six years without hearing about this place?"

Max noticed her cheeks were flushed. When she let down her guard, her stern facade softened. "Well, for starters, he doesn't advertise."

"Why not?"

Max laughed and took a drink of his Scotch. "Well," he began, "Leo's unique. He's wonderful and has a heart as big as the national debt. But he retired some years ago and he's done some screwy things since then. Leo's Landing is one of them."

"But it's a wonderful place! What's screwy about that?"

Max lifted the bottle of wine from the bucket and poured Jane another glass. "Oh, it's wonderful all right. You won't find food this good anywhere. He has the best chef in Chicago, pays him a fortune, and no one is ever disappointed."

"Well, then why—"

"Because the place loses at least a hundred grand a year."

Jane's eyes widened.

"It's the world's worst investment, at least the way Leo runs it. And he doesn't give a hoot. He has fun here, greets his friends, practically supports a soup kitchen down the street with his leftover poulets and vichyssoise and what have you. Sometimes he closes this place for a month or so to give his people here a rest. He closed once to have an Irish wake in here when a bartender's father died. It lasted three days. Anyway, that sort of thing doesn't exactly encourage clientele. But Leo doesn't give a damn. His friends'll come back; that's enough for him."

Jane listened carefully. She wondered if Max knew how much of himself he revealed in talking about his uncle. "How can Leo afford to lose that much money?" she asked.

"Oh, it's not a problem," Max said simply. "And it makes him happy, as well as a whole bunch of other people, so what the hell, I say."

"Well, Leo is crazy about you. That shows."

"It's mutual," Max said. "He's all the family I have." Max paused for a minute as if weighing his words. Then he went on. "Leo was surprised to see you. I don't bring women in here often."

"Why not?"

"Like I said, it's home. Bringing someone here is a little too close to asking for approval. Even at my age, Leo considers himself a sort of ancient patriarch."

Jane laughed. "So Leo is probably standing over the soup this minute, writing a report."

"No. He's probably resting in a battered leather chair he keeps in his office and writing it there."

"You should tell him, Max."

"Tell him what?"

He was watching her so closely that Jane felt her skin tingle. Goose bumps pressed against the silky material of her blouse. A warm pool of unnerving pleasure collected between her legs. She took a sip of her wine and swallowed it quickly. "Well," she said finally, "tell him that this is strictly business, that no screening is necessary." Somewhere in the background a piano player had begun playing light jazz, and Jane felt the music float around inside her.

Max was still looking at her, his blue eyes reading into her thoughts. He leaned forward and rested his forearms on the table. "Oh, it's okay," he said. "Leo will think what he wants to, no matter what I tell him. And I could tell you'd already passed."

Jane was having trouble focusing on his words. He was watching her in an unnervingly personal way, the way she looked at Dewey when trying to figure out what he was feeling and thinking. She reached for her wineglass and saw that her hand was shaking, so she put it back down on the tabletop.

Max saw the emotions move across her face. "Jane," he asked, "are you all right?"

His eyes didn't change, but his voice was gentle and deep. Jane fought the feelings that were nearly overwhelming now. Finally she looked up at him. "Yes, thank you. I felt a little woozy for a minute, but I'm fine now." She reached for the water glass and managed to sip it without spilling any. "Much better."

Max watched her, his concern touched with curiosity. Though she tried hard to hide her feelings, when it came to basic things like desire, Max couldn't be misled.

Jane switched from water to wine and collected herself. Now she felt anger, anger at Max because he didn't tell a joke, or stop looking at her, or leave to go to the men's room so she could gracefully pull herself back together. It was plainly irrational anger but queerly comforting just the same. And easier to manage than whatever else it was she was feeling.

The waiter arrived then with bowls of rich mushroom soup. Jane silently thanked Uncle Leo for his timing.

"Was I right?" Max was smiling, his voice back to the normal rich tones minus the sensuality that had caused Jane's heart to skip a beat.

"Oh, about the soup!" Jane said. "Yes, absolutely. This is wonderful."

"Don't say anything to Leo because he'll tell you at great length how he braved packs of greedy, dangerous morel hunters to personally pluck the prized mushrooms from their hiding places."

Jane noticed that the web of tiny laugh lines around Max's eyes deepened when he talked. She was drifting again. She must be tired. With difficulty she switched her attention from his face to his words. "Leo hunts mushrooms?"

"No. Leo *says* he hunts mushrooms. He really gets them through a food broker. Or his manager does."

"Well, wherever they come from, the soup is great. And the piano player, and the whole place."

"So you're glad you stayed?"

Jane thought about that for a minute. It didn't make sense to deny the fact that she was enjoying the whole evening. She looked into Max's face. "Yes, I'm glad I stayed. This is wonderful. Thank you."

When the main course came, they both fell silent for a while and concentrated on giving Leo's special scallop dish its honest due. By the time the peach flambé was set in front of them, flaming on a wide oval platter, Jane had convinced herself that she was able to relax due to the fact that this wasn't a date and Max wasn't a suitor. He was a client. Someone neutral. Yes, she thought, finding comfort in the logical explanation. And with absolute determination she ignored the tingling nerve endings throughout her body that were telling her there was absolutely nothing neutral about Max Harris.

Leo had left long before Max and Jane walked back through the bar and out into the night. "I didn't get to thank him," Jane said.

"That's okay. He always assumes people will come back. And they always do. You can thank him then."

"Max—"

"Jane—"

"Ladies first," Max said with a slight bow.

Jane met his clear-eyed gaze. "Oh, I wasn't going to say anything important. Except that this *was* nice, Max. I enjoyed it, the whole thing."

But, Max thought silently. There was a definite *but* on the end of that sentence. Jane wanted him to know that the evening, as nice as it was, wouldn't be repeated. He waited for her to continue, but she fell silent, her gaze dropping to the sidewalk.

"Well, good. That's good, Jane," he said softly. He wanted to reach out and touch her. She looked so damn vulnerable standing there like that, this competent professional lady who somehow, sometime, had been made to be afraid. He wanted to tell her it would be okay. One dinner did not make pain. And then he frowned at the absurdity of the thought.

"I need to get home now," Jane said.

"Sure." Max took her elbow, and Jane allowed him to walk her back to the parking lot.

"Well, I have everything I need," she said, patting her briefcase, then slipping behind the wheel of her neat, faded ten-year-old car.

Max didn't think that was true, not by a long shot. Jane Barnett needed loving.

"So," she said, and smiled through the open door, "thanks for putting it all together for me. I should have your returns to you in a week or two."

Max just nodded. He couldn't take his eyes off her, and words suddenly seemed very lacking. He wanted to kiss her. He wanted to do more than kiss her. And it wasn't just the sexual attraction. Something stirred inside of him, something that he thought had died ten years ago. He closed the door firmly, then managed a smile through the closed window. He stood there for a minute, watching the taillights disappear.

An accountant, he thought, and a slow smile spread across his face. Leo was right. Life was filled with the damnedest surprises.

Three

Max knew they'd meet again even though Jane had finished his forms with efficient haste and returned them in the mail. She'd enclosed instructions as to where he should sign before mailing the papers to the IRS, a two-sentence thank you for the dinner and her bill. She'd effectively wiped away any reason for them to get together. But it didn't matter; it would happen in spite of her careful planning.

This feeling of an inevitable meeting was slightly eerie. Karma, maybe, Max told his dog, Potter, as they made their daily runs along Lake Michigan. Uncle Leo sensed it, too, claiming he could feel it in his arthritic bones. The lovely Jane, he said, was not to exit so hastily from their lives.

Even so, Max was surprised at the meeting fate arranged.

Max looked in the car mirror to straighten the black bow tie just below his chin. He didn't much like bow ties and he felt more like a penguin than an ersatz croupier. But he would get the job done.

A young valet stepped out of an attentive line of uniformed young men, but Max drove on by him and parked his car at the end of the circle drive. This particular job was a favor for an acquaintance, and he hoped to get away early.

"Favor" jobs seemed to be filling his days lately, he thought as he walked back toward the club. It was time he stopped taking on jobs because one of Leo's regulars had a great-aunt with a problem or the guy who lived above him didn't know who else to call. He'd moved into this kind of work so he could pick and choose his jobs, and one of these days he'd start doing just that. Yeah, he decided, smoothing back a troublesome lock of hair, this just might be his last favor. Then he laughed, knowing that day would never come. Favors made the world go round.

Max walked into the private club where the party was being held. The elegant rooms had been transformed into Caesar's Palace for the North Shore charity gala, and even Max was impressed. He asked a distinguished white-haired gentleman where the casino staff was meeting, and then, following the man's directions, wove his way through the sea of tables toward a meeting room located in the back of the club. There he found several other men and women in black-tie practicing their deals.

There'd been a rash of robberies on the North Shore recently, all at elegant parties like this one. One of the insurance companies was getting a little testy. The catering company used at all the parties was the same, and it was decided they needed a little checking out.

Going as one of the croupiers was Max's idea. He thought it would be a lot more fun than going as a guest. And after an hour and a half at the table, he knew he'd made the right decision. In fact, he was beginning to wonder if perhaps he'd missed his calling. There was a certain pleasure in shuffling the cards in a neat, precise rhythm, then scooping them back into his hand. He was having such a good time that the couple of breaks he'd taken to check on things in the kitchen and elsewhere were taken halfheartedly. He had done his job though and was nearly certain he had the case wrapped up. Everyone would be happy, including Leo's barber's brother-in-law, who was part-owner of the insurance company.

Now Max was free to concentrate on more important things, like dealing out jacks and aces and the queen of hearts. He looked up to smile at a beautiful silvery-blond player.

And then he saw her.

All the anxiety that had been needling Max for days mushroomed into a huge tidal wave. The cards slipped from his hand and scattered across the green felt surface.

The blond frowned at him.

Max collected himself, flashed the woman a broad smile, and expertly scooped up the cards. And then, while he rhythmically placed the cards in front of the waiting players, his gaze travelled across the room.

Jane stood alone at a pair of French doors. She was dressed in a blue silk gown that clung to her figure and stirred Max's blood. She looked regal, cool, distant and vulnerable all at once. The odd combination pulled at him from a million different directions. He scanned the people around her. There were several men and women standing in the group, but it was hard to tell whom she was with. Both the men and women, with the exception of Jane, were society types with large smiles and indiscriminate hugs. Jane stood slightly apart, her eyes seemingly not focused on anything. Now and then she'd enter into the conversation, and then unobtrusively back away, her attention drawn to the soft string music coming from a balcony.

She'd done something different with her hair tonight, Max noticed. It was still pulled back but was formed into an elegant roll down the back of her head. Max thought of Grace Kelly in some old movie he had seen years before about a thief on the Riviera. There was that same look about Jane, that frozen passion that needed to be melted, that untouchable, unforgettable beauty.

Max began to deal another hand and tried to concentrate. He was getting carried away fantasizing about his passionate accountant.

A slight pressure on his arm caused Max to shift gears. A young smiling man told him it was time for his break. Max nodded, slipped his deck of cards into a drawer, and started across the room toward the French doors.

She was gone. He looked across the tops of carefully coiffed heads and around the shoulders of black-suited men. Vanished. Max shrugged off the disappointment. Just as well, maybe. He'd find Jane later if she was still here, but he did need to finish this job. He was, after all, being paid to catch a thief tonight.

The club kitchen was nearly empty, and Max poured himself a mug of thick, black coffee and sat down at a back table to make some notes. The couple of caterers entering the kitchen from the other door didn't see him in the shadows and because they didn't, their voices carried across the pots and pans and trays of half-eaten hors d'oeuvres to where Max slowly drank his coffee. Max listened and wrote, and in less time than it had taken him to master his croupier's poker face, he not only had the insurance company's problems solved, but he had learned that silver and diamonds could be fit into cream puffs and false chocolate cakes quite easily.

When he returned to the festive, noisy party he almost felt guilty. Being paid for jobs that fell into place as easily as this one had didn't seem quite cricket. Everyone, with the notable exception of the Gala Gourmet Catering Company, would be happy, and they wouldn't have to know how easy it had been. Finding Jane Barnett, however, was a bit more difficult.

Max took up his comfortable spot behind the table, set his face in an expressionless mask, and began to deal out the cards. If it really was his karma, he'd find her again. Or she'd find him. Now *that* was a nice thought.

Across the room, behind a potted fern that rose several inches beyond her five feet six inches, Jane stood in a shadow, enjoying the solitude. Plants she could deal with; it was the crowd she was avoiding. She'd come to the party simply to get her close friend, Sara Jennings, off her back. Sara had used business as an enticement: "You'll make contacts that will bring in new clients, Jane. Think of it as advertising and soccer camp for Dewey."

Jane ran her hand down the smooth, snug-fitting silk dress. The Yellow Pages, she decided, was a better bet for business growth. She didn't consider herself antisocial, but these kinds of galas were far too reminiscent of a life she'd left behind her forever. Even the bank executive who had escorted her touched cords of discontent. He was young and brash and on his way up, just as Craig had been. Jane was simply a part of the evening's accoutrements, like his tux and his flashy smile. He probably didn't even notice that she'd been absent from his side for nearly an hour now.

She pushed a single errant hair back into place and took a deep breath. The music was beautiful and there was a breeze blowing in from the lake. She'd concentrate on that.

Suddenly she froze. Directly opposite her, positioned between the two longest fronds of the fern, was Max Harris's double. Except he wasn't a gumshoe, he was a croupier. Jane spread the fronds apart with her hands and stared at him. He was dealing cards and looking at a tall, elegant black-haired woman whose diamond pendant hung between two prominent breasts. The woman said something, and the croupier smiled. Jane gasped. It was that same, slightly lopsided, heart-stopping smile. This wasn't Max's double; this was Max.

Jane found herself smiling, too. She had a wonderful view of him. He must be on a job, she thought, and then she wondered what he would manage to deduct from his taxes for this job. The thought made her smile. *Max* made her smile. The sight of him caused ripples of pleasure to move through her, washing away her discomfort. She'd not been able to forget the handsome, easygoing man, even though her instincts told her forgetting him was the safest course. The problem with Max was that he listened to her too closely and when he looked at her with those incredible all-seeing eyes, she felt him touch her soul. And that was more than Jane wanted to deal with.

Max laughed now at something someone at his table said, and she could almost hear the deep-throated sound across the mass of bodies and elegant gowns. She smiled again, and at that moment he looked up. His eyes met hers.

Jane instinctively tried to hide her smile, but it refused to budge. Max grinned. His brows lifted, and he waved. Several people followed his gaze, puzzled. Max didn't notice. Without taking his eyes from her, he snagged the arm of a passing fellow worker and convinced him he belonged behind the table.

Jane watched his lips form the word "urgent" as he spoke to the man.

And then he wound his way through the throngs of people until he stood at her side.

He didn't touch her, although he wanted to. Her smooth, bare shoulders appeared luminous, and he longed to run his fingers over the silken surface. But he held back, cautioning himself carefully. He had found her, but she was like a young deer, so easily frightened off. He smiled down into her face. "Hi," he said.

Jane felt unexpectedly glad to see him. There was no sane, logical explanation for her feelings, but Jane suddenly found herself not caring. "Hi, Max. What are you doing here?"

"I was working, dealing cards. And then I looked up and saw you standing here with only a plant to enjoy your beauty. It seemed a damn shame." He fingered the tip of the frond as he talked, and Jane laughed at his charming words.

"So," Max went on, "I thought to myself, 'Max, there she is, an enchanting stranger, across the crowded room.'" His laughing eyes gazed down on her, and Jane shook her head and dazzled him with a free, open smile.

"You're a little crazy, Max Harris."

"Ah, the lady likes me." He pounded his heart with his fist. Her whole being changed when she smiled so openly; Max wanted the smile to last forever.

Jane shook her head a little as if to refute his words. But then she stopped and nodded. "I like you, Max. And I'm glad you're here."

He leaned over and whispered conspiratorially in her ear. "I'm hired help, Jane. Does that change things?"

"Yes. It makes you the most desirable man in the room."

"The unexpected perks of dealing cards are nice." Max slipped an arm across her shoulders and led her around the plant and over to a love seat on the other side.

"Are you on a case?" Jane asked.

"Was. I solved it on my break. The butler didn't do it."

Jane laughed. "Do I want to know who did?"

Max shrugged. "I dunno, Jane, it's pretty devastating." He cocked his head to one side and looked at her with a lopsided smile. "But you look like a strong woman. Okay." He paused dramatically. "It was the cream puffs."

Jane shook her head. "I never did trust cream puffs," she said.

A waiter passed by, and Max lifted two glasses of champagne from the tray. Jane took the glass and sipped it slowly.

Behind her, beyond the windows, a moon cast slanted beams across her shoulders. The effect brought Max pleasure. He brought his eyes back to her face. "Speaking of mysteries, you seem to be alone—"

"No. But the gentleman I'm with seems to have disappeared. I haven't seen him for nearly two hours."

"Too bad," Max said.

"Yes." Jane smoothed an imaginary wrinkle from the blue silk of her dress. Max's closeness was comforting and nerve-racking all at the same time. Jane was used to feeling alone in a crowd. It was a feeling she didn't shy away from because it brought her an odd sense of security. But Max Harris's presence disturbed that aloneness in a way Jane wasn't used to. She liked having Max next to her; maybe that was the problem.

She glanced at her watch. "It's late," she said. "I'd better find my escort."

Max thought fast. "There's quite a crowd here. Let me help." He stood, then looked down at her and smiled crookedly. "Actually, Jane, I'll give you a choice."

"Oh?"

"You can hire me to find this guy," Max continued. "I'm pretty good at that sort of thing. Or let me take you home. I'm leaving anyway. The last option's by far the least expensive."

"Your chauffeuring services are cheaper than investigations?"

"Well, I don't know. I have a feeling there's nothing cheap about any of this."

His cryptic remark echoed her feelings. But when he reached for her hand, she rose automatically from the couch. Her heart was beating erratically.

Max continued. "I really would like to help if I can, and I'd most definitely like to leave. The solution is to leave here with you."

"I ought to at least see if he's looking for me. My escort, I mean." Jane was flustered. She felt a quick rush of color rise to her cheeks. She was suddenly acutely aware of her body. As she walked with Max across the room she hoped he wouldn't look at her, because if he did he'd have to see it, too; a sensuality as strong as hers could not be hidden.

"You look beautiful tonight, you know."

Max's voice was deep and rich against the harsher noises of the party. Jane took in a quick breath. Max was weaving in and out of the mass of party goers and didn't seem to be looking at her as he spoke. He went on. "I mean it, Jane. You're a spectacular-looking woman."

And you're a spectacular-looking man, she wanted to say.

Instead she said, "Thank you," and slowed one step so his quick sideways glances didn't land on her.

"You're welcome. And personally I think your date must have a screw loose to leave you alone for this long. We'll give a look on our way out, but if we see him, I think a polite 'so-long' is all he deserves." Max took her elbow and guided her quickly through the club. No one noticed them, no one sought Jane out and Max had her out the front door before she could suggest checking the upper level. He left a message with the doorman in case anyone asked for Jane, and the two hurried down the front steps, hand in hand.

"I feel like a kid," Jane said with just a touch of embarrassment. "Ditching a date—"

"It seems to have been a mutual ditching."

"He's probably in the bar doing some business. He won't miss me, I'm sure, but whether he does or not isn't really the point. I usually don't act this way."

"Maybe I'm a bad influence on you. Or maybe I'm a good influence on you. What d'ya think?"

Jane looked up at him. Beyond his handsome, teasing face, the moon was shining brightly. She smiled and collected her thoughts. "I think I want to leave."

"I think so, too," Max said.

The light from the moon caught the shadow of a dimple in one cheek when he smiled. "So, he said, we're out of here—" The end of his sentence was nearly blocked out by a sudden rumbling coming from his stomach.

"Obviously you didn't eat the cream puffs."

"Couldn't," Max said, putting one hand over the source of the noise. "Evidence. But I'm starving. Did you eat in there?"

Jane shook her head no. Max was holding open the door to his well cared for 1968 sports car, and she slipped into the front seat.

"Me, either," he called out as he rounded the car and got in beside her. "In fact I haven't eaten for hours. Maybe days."

Jane laughed.

"Could I talk you into stopping at Sadie's on the way home?"

"It's late, Max . . ."

Max purposely misunderstood her words. He'd decided back beside the potted fern that, as competent as Jane Barnett was, she wasn't nearly as sure of her own mind as she was of numbers. "It's never too late for Sadie. She never closes. And you'll love her, Jane, not to mention her flapjacks."

Jane didn't answer. The tiredness from the long evening was settling in, aided along by the champagne on an empty stomach. She hadn't eaten all day either; Saturdays were busy, and there hadn't been time. Dewey had needed a haircut, the lawn had to be cut and the house cleaned, and she'd also managed to squeeze in a couple of hours in her office after Dewey had left for the Jennings. There were never enough hours, never enough time... Jane closed her eyes and rested her head back against the seat.

Max glanced over at her. "You really are tired, aren't you?" He hesitated. "Maybe I should get you home."

Jane shook her head and smiled in the darkness. "No, it's okay. Food sounds good. I'm not so sure about flapjacks, but—"

"How do you feel about grits?"

Jane laughed. "Well, I'm sure there'll be something."

They drove in comfortable silence along the lake and then headed west just north of downtown. Max slowed, then stopped the car, and Jane opened her eyes. They were parked in front of an all-night diner, exactly like the kind she'd seen in movies. It was long and narrow with square windows lit with yellow lights. Truckers wearing worn leather jackets sat hunched over their food, and through the smudged panes of the door Jane could hear music.

"Didn't I tell you it was great?" Max said as he held open the door.

It wasn't until the six or so other diners all looked up and stared at them that it occurred to Jane what they looked like, she in her elegant formal, and Max handsome and dashing in his tux.

One of the men whistled through stained teeth, and Max gave the man a comical bow, accepting the gesture meant for Jane and warding off her embarrassment. Quickly he ushered her across the patterned linoleum floor to a booth. "Your table, madam."

His smile gave her a sense of well-being, made her feel that it was okay for her to be there in the dingy diner at midnight, dressed to the hilt.

A round waitress who looked nearly as old as Uncle Leo took their order. Before Max had a chance to ask after Sadie, she went on to tell him that Sadie was in Peoria at a family reunion but would be forever grateful to Max for tracing down those old stock certificates for her. They'd paid off and she was going to get new gutters for the restaurant.

Jane listened to the exchange curiously. Max could never be accused of being ordinary. Not in professions, nor friends nor tax deductions. Jane was used to the ordinary; she was comfortable and happy with it, but Max Harris was ushering a fresh breeze into her life that felt surprisingly good. She just hoped that when it stopped blowing, there wouldn't be any damage done.

Max hooked a finger beneath his bow tie and pulled it off, then unbuttoned the top of his stiff white shirt. In a second his jacket was off and his sleeves rolled halfway up to his elbows. "There." His sigh was exaggerated, his smile meant to put Jane at ease. "Much better. Now, tell me, Jane—what was a nice girl like you doing at that extravaganza?"

"Actually, I spent a lot of time tonight asking myself the same thing."

"You didn't enjoy it?" He had known that from watching her. But the irony was that Jane fit into the elegant group of party goers as well as or better than anyone there. Max suspected she wasn't new to the country club scene.

"I guess I'm not a party person," Jane said. "I went because my friend thought it would be good for me—for business if I socialized more. But I think there are easier ways."

"Much. But it worked out okay. I think it was fate, your being there. When I spotted you standing across the room, I felt a kind of reprieve. The night shifted from murky black to midnight blue in the blink of an eye."

Jane found it easy to accept the exaggerated compliment easily. It was the way he dished it out, she guessed, as naturally as breathing. He watched her as he spoke to her, reading her reaction but even that didn't bother her. It was a kind, nonthreatening look.

She'd been attracted to Max Harris almost from the first, but those vague stirrings of sexual intimacy made Jane uneasy. Her psychologist had told her it was a pattern of withdrawal from men that was not at all uncommon given the circumstances of Jane's marriage. And with hard work the pattern could be broken. It would get better. For the first time in a long while, Jane felt a rush of hope that maybe the woman who had listened and counseled her for all those months might be right.

"You're smiling," Max said.

Jane shook her head and lowered her eyes, then lifted them to speak. "It's us being here like this. It's sort of funny, but also nice."

The arrival of the round waitress with a loaded tray of hot, mouth-watering food saved her from further explanation. Max had ordered everything but the kitchen sink, and Jane laughed out loud as the small table was filled with platters of eggs, bacon and puffy hotcakes with thick maple syrup. There were side orders of crunchy hashbrowns, a basket of homemade blueberry muffins and a fat carafe of hot, steaming coffee. "Everything's as fresh as Max here," the waitress announced to Jane, and then she padded away on her crepe-soled shoes.

Max laughed. "Ruby's great. She and Sadie are sisters. Great ladies." Then the enticing aroma of the food stopped his idle talk quickly, and he dug in while Jane watched with wide blue-green eyes.

Between bites and slow drinks from the fat porcelain mug Ruby kept filled, Jane watched Max eat. His wide shoulders were bent over the plate, his dark head bowed. Large, sure hands held the silverware, and she could almost feel the satisfaction in his body.

He looked up and saw her watching him. "I like to eat," he said with a grin.

"I noticed. But where does it go? You're in terrific shape." The words slipped out unintentionally as she examined his magnificently proportioned body.

Max knew without looking up that she probably regretted the Freudian slip. He lifted his head, and before she could try to take back the words, he flashed a grin and said, "This tuxedo does wonders." And then he pointed to her plate and frowned fiercely. "I don't think I need to tell you what Ruby does with no-eaters."

Jane half smiled. "The choices stymied me. At this time of night it's tough to decide—"

"To decide everything?"

"Anything," she said hastily, wondering why she felt the conversation had taken a sharp left turn.

"Then let's make it eggs."

"Just what I was thinking." She proved it by piling a generous helping of scrambled eggs on her plate. She was surprised at how hungry she was, and even the feel of Max's clear blue eyes on her didn't slow her down.

Jane had never tasted better scrambled eggs.

By the time Jane got home that night, she knew that in the length of time it took to throw a fancy party on the North Shore of Chicago, her twenty-nine-year-long life had changed. She could now share with a man, she could touch and enjoy a man and she could be filled with heart-stirring pleasure from the contact. And she could accomplish all that with only a small, nearly manageable amount of fear.

Four

The small boy skidded to a stop in front of the mirror. He stood on tiptoe and peered into the glass, then brushed a thick strand of dishwater blond hair back off his forehead. "There," he said with great satisfaction.

"No, Dewey," Jane said from the other side of the room. "Use a comb." She checked the contents of her purse, then grabbed a light linen jacket from the back of a chair.

Dewey remained in front of the mirror, his brows drawn together until they almost touched. Then he crossed his eyes behind the large dark-rimmed glasses and laughed out loud at the image that stared back at him.

"Dewey, don't do that."

"Okay," he said cheerfully, and bounded out the front door to sit on the steps and wait for the Jennings to arrive.

Jane watched his body fly through the door and wondered briefly why kids weren't studied in physics classes; they certainly defied most of the laws. She watched Dewey bend at the waist now; his nose was just inches from the cement and his glasses slid down the short expanse of nose as he observed something— a bug or caterpillar or ant, Jane supposed—on the sidewalk. Without conscious effort her heart swelled as she watched him. He was her light and her joy and the force that made sense out of a murky, questionable world.

His face lit up now as the bug started to move, and Jane saw the dimples flash in his cheeks. Dewey's face was a constant reflection of passing wonders and miracles. Jane had been approached once about having Dewey do advertising and some modeling jobs and she had been surprised. She thought Dewey was a great looking kid, of course, just as all mothers did of their own kids. But this wasn't the commercial kind of good looks, not the kind demanded by the public. The talent agent had disagreed. Dewey's was a fresh, beguiling look, he said, a unique look, one that would make people remember the product because they'd remember the intriguing kid who grinned when seated in front of a colorful bowl of Jello or sighed delightedly as his mother handed him fresh smelling jeans.

Jane of course had said no and had said it so forcefully that it had sent the agent scurrying to get away from the fierce, irrational mother who couldn't see the dollar signs her son's looks represented.

Jane didn't want a childhood career for Dewey. All she wanted for the son she loved more than her own life was a safe and secure existence and a bright, happy future. And those hopes she tended and nurtured as carefully as the world's most prized garden.

"They're here!" Dewey screeched.

Startled from her thoughts, Jane slipped the strap of her purse over her shoulder and hurried out into the fading sunlight.

She wasn't sure why she was taking her two closest friends in the world and her six-year-old son to Leo's Landing. She'd told George and Sara Jennings that it was because of the food—wonderful, homemade dinners that they'd love. But it wasn't the food that Jane thought about when she remembered her night at Leo's place. It was the hint of laughter in Max's bottomless blue eyes and his gentle ways. She had thought about Max a lot these past couple of weeks.

When he had called after the casino party and suggested a real "date," Jane had turned him down. After the night spent in the diner, she knew without question that Max's entry into her life couldn't be a casual one. It would be the kind that demanded something from her. And as much as she liked him, she didn't think she could chance making herself vulnerable.

She had nearly weakened when she'd heard his voice. It was already like an old, familiar song to her. But the voice of reason won, and she told Max that she couldn't go out with him. From his response she knew he assumed there was probably someone else in the picture. And she let him believe that because there was no reason not to.

And then she had gone on with her life, trying to ignore the very real presence of Max Harris, who was refusing to leave her thoughts.

"Are we on the right street?" Sara Jennings asked over the front seat of the BMW.

Jane scanned the street numbers. "Yes. Just a few more blocks."

"Now tell me once more how we stumbled on this gourmet treasure?" It was George speaking this time, his chin lifting as he sought Jane in the rearview mirror.

"A...a client. I met a client at this place to exchange some papers."

"Eating out with clients now, are we?" Sara asked brightly.

"We had some unfinished business, and he suggested we meet here. It was convenient."

"How old?" Sara asked.

"Oh, old, very old. It used to be a warehouse, I think."

"The client, Jane. How old is the male client?"

"Oh, I don't know," she lied. And then, feeling guilty at doing so in front of Dewey, she said, "He's thirty-six."

"Nice," said George.

"What's so nice about it?" Jane asked.

"It's nice because that's my age. Thirty-six is a dependable age. Good. Solid."

"Not according to a book I've read," said Sara.

"You can't believe everything you read, butter-cup," said George, and when he stopped at the light he leaned over and pecked his wife of seven years on the cheek.

Jane laughed. "You two are hopeless."

"Hopeless, shmopeless," echoed Dewey, who had been busy counting convertibles.

"Right," said Jane, drawing her son into her side. She breathed in the clean soapy smell of Dewey's hair and skin.

It was a perfect spring night, the kind that sent Chicagoans by the droves out into the evening air. Michigan Avenue's sidewalks were filled with strollers stopping to look into the expensive shop windows or idling in the small park near the old water tower where a band was playing familiar show tunes. Jane breathed in the air that blew in off the lake and through the open window, and she felt an almost overwhelming sense of harmony and well-being. She looked down at Dewey and saw that he was watching her.

When their eyes met, Dewey frowned. "Okay, Mom, what's up?"

Jane laughed. "Can't I smile for no reason?"

Dewey shook his head until his neatly combed blond hair fell in a sweep across his forehead, and then they both laughed and Dewey scooted back over to the window and concentrated on a group of brightly dressed dancers, who were performing on a street corner. His mother's strange mood was soon forgotten.

"What does he do?" Sara asked from the front seat.

"Who?"

"The client, the client!"

Jane sat back in the leather seat and laughed softly.

Sara had turned around and folded her arms across the back of the seat, resting her chin on her forearms and focusing her hazel eyes intently on Jane's face. "I want the real poop, Janie." Dewey laughed delightedly at Sara's choice of words.

"He has a small business," Jane said finally.

Sara turned back and looked at George with such hope and approval that Jane couldn't help but laugh. "Sara, when will you give up?"

"Never," Sara said sweetly. She looked over at Dewey, who was now picking out words from neon signs. Then she looked back at Jane and mouthed her words. "I think the only thing that will completely erase the damage done by that basta—"

"Sara..." Jane warned, her body shifting as she sought to protect Dewey in its curve.

"I know, I know. As I was saying, a man in your life wouldn't be all bad, my dear friend."

"There's no room in the inn," Jane said, and then she concentrated on a glimpse of the lake to hide the emotion in her face. She had thought for such a long time that she would never, ever allow a man back in her life. There was no need for one. A man had nearly destroyed her. Men made her feel threatened. George Jennings was an exception, but he was taken.

But thoughts of Max Harris seemed to fill the silence in the car, and Jane wondered for a minute why Sara didn't sense them.

This time Jane wasn't even surprised when the faint stirrings of pleasure began.

Max sat at the bar and stirred his Scotch with a thin, red swizzle stick. Uncle Leo stood behind him, his arms clamped solidly across his thick belly, and watched him closely, "You want to know what I think Max?"

"No, Leo."

"I think this spring is bringing out the birds and the bees and they're buzzing right in your ear."

Max laughed, and Leo continued. "And I think it's the lovely Jane, the woman with the smile of an angel, who's doing it to you."

"She does have a nice smile. Cautious, but nice."

"See, Leo knows."

"Then Leo also knows I'm not looking for an angel with a nice smile. They turn into wives—"

"And give worthy men nephews!"

"Hey, Leo, you've got me, don't you?"

"You don't bounce so great on the knee."

"Well, you may have to settle for Potter. The lovely Jane turned me down for a date. Besides, I'm not really in the market, Leo. You know that."

"What I know, Max, is that being responsible for someone again scares the hair off your chest. And I know, I understand. I was there, Max." Leo's square hand landed heavily on Max's shoulder.

"Then why all this talk about Jane, Leo?"

Leo shook his head. "I don't know, except sometimes you go to market even if you think you don't need anything, because it's the only time the best produce will be there. You know?" He patted Max on the shoulder and then was called away to settle a kitchen dispute.

Max watched him walk away. His uncle was a good man and as perceptive as hell. Max thought about what Leo had said. Jane was on his mind more than he wanted to admit. He wanted to see her again, but not the way he usually wanted to see women again. For a while he hadn't been sure how it was different. Max knew a lot of women, had satisfying affairs with some, nice friendships with others.

But none of them had the effect on him that his accountant was having. His recent dreams were eerie, an omen of sorts. Some of his friends thought it was odd that he didn't dream, but it wasn't nearly as odd to Max as the technicolor videos taking place when he closed his eyes these nights.

They weren't all about Jane; some were simply about himself, soaring high on clouds and mountaintops and beneath helium balloons. The sky was always blue and deep, the feeling always nice and hopeful.

Then when Jane came into the picture, brilliant fiery sunsets filled the sky, and afterwards, in a star-studded galaxy, the peace was so profound that it woke him up one night. The dreams...The dreams were building an incongruous bridge between himself and a woman he barely knew.

Max swallowed the last of his drink and slid off the tall stool. He probably needed food. Sometimes he got a little crazy in his thoughts when his stomach was waging war.

Music from a baby grand piano filtered into the bar from the back dining room, and Max followed it, hoping he'd find an empty table where he could sit alone and figure out the meaning of life.

Uncle Leo smiled at Max from across the room, and then headed his way. But before he could reach him, Max spotted the foursome.

They were sitting near the window, not far from where he and Jane had sat that first night. It was Jane and a family—two adults and a small boy whose back was to him. The intimate group seemed happy and relaxed and chatted with quiet animation while Max watched.

"So nice for her to come here, Max. She likes us," Leo said at his elbow.

Max didn't speak for a moment; he was analyzing the emotion that ran through him. He grinned. Hell, here he was at thirty-six—with butterflies.

"More beautiful than before, yes?"

"Yes," Max said, his eyes not leaving Jane's face. The candles on the table cast a glow over her, and her cheekbones were highlighted. For a minute she took his breath away. Then he asked, "Do you know who she's with?"

"Friends. The Jennings is how she introduced them. And the little one is Dewey. They just arrived."

Max nodded. "Okay, thanks Leo. I think I'll say hello." And without checking on Leo's grin that Max suspected stretched clear from one ear to the other, he wove his way through the linen-draped tables until he stood at Jane's elbow.

"Hello, Jane."

Jane had been listening to one of George's exaggerated accounts of life in the fast track world of advertising, and the voice startled her. Slowly she turned her head. Her eyes met Max's.

"Max! Well, hello."

Max wanted to keep looking at Jane, but he finally managed to take in the rest of the table, smiling as Jane introduced him to the attractive woman with the wavy red hair and her husband, George, a friendly man with an open face and ready smile, and then to the little boy. Dewey, Jane had called him.

He looked at Dewey once, and then again. There was something familiar about his features. Or maybe it was the clear, level look he gave Max. Far too level and clear for his age, Max thought. "Hi," the boy said with a slow smile. "Are you the client?"

"The client?" Max said, amused.

"*Mom's* client," Dewey said. "You found us this place. It's cool. I can see tugboats down there. And some algae, and there's some dead fish over there. It's the greatest place to eat so far." He pointed a stubby finger out the window at the dock that hugged the riverfront below.

Max listened but lost the end of the sentence. *Mom's client.* That's what was familiar about Dewey. He wasn't the Jennings child; he was *Jane's* son, and his eyes were his mother's, that color green as soft as spring grass. The only difference was that the vulnerability and caution in Jane's eyes were absent, replaced by a child's innocent eagerness for anything new.

Conflicting emotions welled up in Max. Jane had given him no indication that she had a son. And even now he sensed in her a reluctance to grant him knowledge of the little boy. Max tried to push the disturbing thoughts aside long enough to smile into the child's open stare. "Yeah, the client. I guess maybe I am. I brought your mom here once when she helped me with my taxes."

"I hate taxes," Dewey announced firmly.

Jane smoothed out her napkin. "Taxes mean his mom's real busy," she explained, dodging Max's inquisitive eyes. "Dewey doesn't really hate taxes."

"Well, I do," said Sara. "And I also hate to look miles up in the air when I'm talking to someone." She smiled openly at Max. "Won't you join us for dinner, Max?"

George seconded the invitation with clear enthusiasm. Max glanced at Jane. She was sipping wine, her expression lost in the shadow. George pulled another chair over to the table without waiting for an answer, and Dewey grinned up at Max.

Max shrugged. She hadn't said no. "Sure," he said. "I hate to eat alone."

"So, Max," said Sara, "it seems you are *the* client." She winked at Dewey, and he laughed.

"It's a wise man who picks his accountant carefully," George said. "Our Jane's top-notch. You'll be pleased."

"That's an understatement," said Max. "Anyone who can handle my mess is nothing short of incredible. Jane did a terrific job." His smile was for Jane, and she surprised him by returning it. She seemed to have relaxed a little.

"It was a little tricky," she said to the others. "Max ascribes to the grocery sack filing system."

Before George could speak, Sara clamped her hand over his mouth. "He's going to tell you that I use wastebaskets, but don't believe a word he says. Men in advertising don't always see things realistically." She smiled sweetly at George as he began to nibble on the side of her hand. Any awkwardness of having a stranger join their group was wiped away by her homey gesture, and Max relaxed, knowing Sara and George Jennings were happy to have him there, and Jane's feelings on the subject were best left unanalyzed for now.

Jane sat back and watched her friends' easy acceptance of Max. George and Sara were protective of her, a trait that she both appreciated and resented, and the warmth with which they included Max in their circle was unusual. She wasn't sure how she felt about that. She wasn't sure how she felt about any of this, but she couldn't deny that Max's presence gave her a deep pleasure.

She watched Max with her son. He spoke to Dewey in calm, even tones, not talking down to him nor trying to impress him, nor ignoring him. Dewey was quiet at first, but soon responded, showing his acceptance of this stranger at their table by animatedly describing to Max the family of newts that lived in the bathroom off his kitchen. Later he explained in detail an experiment he was conducting with a tomato plant.

Max suggested he use a kind of red-striped worm to aerate the soil, and Dewey grinned in excitement. When Max said he'd get him some, Jane groaned softly. But inside she smiled, and a rush of pleasure as sweet as Leo's honeyed muffins spread through her.

Max listened and talked and shared carefully selected anecdotes of his life as a private investigator. Dewey was openly impressed, and Sara thought it was grand and romantic. With George he discovered a shared love for single-engine planes and telescopes. It was an unusual evening; Max hadn't felt such companionship in a long time. And somewhere in the midst of it all, somewhere between the shared laughter and easy friendship, between the pleasure of the quiet, beautiful woman at his side and between the mushroom soup and spicy delight of Leo's bouillabaisse, Max Harris felt himself falling in love.

Hours later when the restaurant lights dimmed and George had retrieved a sleeping Dewey from Leo's big office chair, the small group stood together at the front door. Moonlight fell through the windows and illuminated their tired, happy figures. They were reluctant to part, to break the invisible web that held them together in the shadows of the restaurant. Sara, with what she later would call a flash of absolute genius, solved the problem. "Max!" she said suddenly, her hazel eyes flashing, "I've got an idea."

George rolled his eyes toward the ceiling. "Oh-oh. Is everyone ready for this?"

Sara ignored him and placed her hand on Max's arm. "Tomorrow we are going to our farm in Wisconsin. Dewey and Jane are coming, and we'd love to have you as well. It's a big, old place, plenty of room. And the fresh air will do you good."

Jane's eyes popped wide open.

George picked up the invitation. "It'd be a great place to use your telescope, Max. No city lights. You're sure welcome to join us."

Sara shot a quick glance at Jane's objecting face and then continued. "We'll put you to work. George needs to fix some rafters in the barn and he has trouble doing it alone."

Jane bit her lip. They were being ridiculous. Sara and George had plenty of workers who could fix their rafters. It was a ruse, a plan, a conniving—

"And we won't take no for an answer," Sara finished.

"Sara," Jane said calmly, "Max probably has other plans. He's a busy person...."

Max watched her and felt her discomfort. She'd enjoyed the evening every bit as much as the rest of them, and he knew it bothered her somehow. "Hey, it's okay," he said softly. And then he laughed and shook George's hand. "Thanks, but maybe another time."

Jane looked up at him, and she saw it was for her he'd turned down the invitation. She felt foolish. Her fear was foolish. She was a grown woman. "No, Max," she said quietly. "Do come."

Jane hoped a spring storm would flood the narrow country roads and the trip would be canceled.

Jane hoped the weekend would be sunny and beautiful, filled with laughter and a man named Max.

Jane wished her heart would be still enough for her to listen to common sense and resolutions she had made a long time ago.

She pushed her hair behind one ear and then threw a pair of jeans into the small overnight bag. She needed to relax, think clearly about one thing at a time. She was feeling pressured. Overload, her psychologist used to call it.

"I'm ready, Mom," Dewey announced. He stood in the doorway, his small feet and most of his legs hidden in cowboy boots Sara and George had given him. He was as proud of the boots as he was of his newts and trained guinea pig. With a grin lighting his small face, he hooked his thumbs into the pockets of his jeans.

Jane melted. There was no such thing as overload. "Okay, sport," she said. "Me, too."

Dewey wrinkled his nose, then spun around on the heels of his boots and flew through the house. Jane watched him until he disappeared from sight. Then she pulled her hair back into a ponytail, tied it quickly with a ribbon and snapped her small suitcase shut.

She looked around her quiet, subdued bedroom; she had worked so hard for peace in her life. She shook her head and walked out to the Jennings' waiting car.

George and Max had sorted out the details of the trip the night before. Max was going to drive up in his own car because he had some reports to drop off with a client on the way. They'd all arrive about the same time it was thought.

When George pulled into the lane that wound up to the sprawling country house, Jane sighed out loud. "This place is heaven."

Beside her, Sara nodded. "Paradise may be more appropriate this weekend."

"Sometimes I wonder why I put up with you," Jane said. With that, they slipped from the car.

"The same reason I put up with you, Jane. Because we're the best of friends. And I hate to say it because I think that lovely, calm temperament of yours will go berserk, but I think you're on the verge of another attachment. Maybe even a soul mate. You only get one of those, you know."

"Sara, I hardly know him."

"True." Sara looped an arm through Jane's as they walked up the stone pathway to the house. "But there's something going on. I feel it, so you sure as hell must."

Jane was silent for a long moment. At last she spoke. "Yes, I feel something. But I don't know, Sara. I'm all right up to a point, but there's a line there, an invisible line—"

"And you don't want to cross over it."

"Yes, that's right. I don't think I *can* cross over it, Sara," she said softly, a touch of sadness in her voice. "It's the trusting...."

Sara stopped in the middle of the pathway. She turned and hugged Jane tightly. "It's okay, Janie. Don't fight it. Let things happen as they will. If trust grows out of it, then that's good. But I know, hon. I know how hard it must be.''

Sara did understand most things, Jane thought. She alone understood the horrors of her past. But there was one thing she couldn't understand because she was so secure and happy in her marriage to George, and that was that Jane didn't need marriage. She didn't need a man. All she needed was Dewey and a safe and secure life.

And no matter what kind of feelings Max Harris stirred inside her, and no matter how kind a person he was, there was always the sad truth that she had once thought Craig Barnett was a kind, nice person.

"Are you two coming in or not?" George asked from the screen door. "Looks like Max isn't here yet."

"Do you think he got lost?" Sara asked.

"Nope, not a chance. I give excellent directions."

"Maybe he decided not to come," Jane said.

"Wrong, Mom!" Dewey announced as he tore across the porch. "There he is!"

In the distance a cloud of dust spiraled up into the air from the dirt road.

"What's he driving?" Sara asked.

Jane cupped her hands over her eyes and squinted against the bright glare of the noontime sun. "A Jeep. He drove all the way up here in a Jeep...."

"*They,*" George corrected.

And when Max circled around the clearing in front of the rambling two-story house and came to a stop, two figures fell out of the mud-splattered vehicle.

"Hi, folks," said Max. "Meet Potter."

Dewey shrieked, and the heels of his cowboy boots clicked against the wooden steps as he flew down to greet the friendly sheepdog who covered his flushed cheeks with long wet licks.

"Potter?" Jane murmured, following Sara and George down the steps.

"George invited him," Max explained. "He loves the country. And terrific little kids." He nodded toward Dewey. The tow-headed boy had wrapped his short arms around the mass of fur and was explaining the day's activities to the dog.

Jane watched her son quietly. "He's never had a dog," she said. "This is a treat for him."

"For Potter, too," Max said. "He's never had a kid for a friend."

"Jane, why don't you show Max around, get him organized," Sara called over to the two of them. "George and I are going to throw some lunch together."

"I'll help," Jane started to say, but Sara had already disappeared. The slam of the screen door shut out arguments.

Max raised his eyebrows.

"It's pretty obvious, isn't it?"

"Yep." Max laughed. "It's kind of nice, though. Sara has obviously known you a long time. And I get the feeling she's pretty protective. I consider her efforts a compliment."

"Except matchmaking is ridiculous. You can't do that."

"Well, probably not. But we might as well make the most of it." Max shoved his hands into his jeans pockets and leaned his head slightly to one side. "I have to admit, Jane—I think spending the weekend here—being here with you—is one of the better uses I've made of weekends in a long time."

Jane looked up into smiling, lined eyes. They were clear and kind and uncomplicated. Surely for two short days she could enjoy herself. Surely she could have an enjoyable, uncomplicated weekend. She smiled to herself in resolution, and when Max looked down at her, she felt seeds of caution scatter about the countryside.

"Well?" Max said.

"Well, I think we better move on with this tour or we'll miss lunch."

"A fate worse than death," Max growled, making Jane laugh. When he took her hand and told her to lead the way, she felt happy.

The day passed by for Jane in a magical blend of colors: the golden noon of exploring the farm with Max, of showing him the barn and the fresh hay and the pond out beyond the thick hedge of wild blackberries, the brilliant red and oranges of sunset that splashed across the sky in front of them as George and Sara, Dewey and Potter, and Jane and Max climbed over the hill to buy some fresh fruit and cheese and eggs from the neighboring farm; and the deep, heart-stirring blue-black of the evening sky as they all stood in the field with the wild grasses rubbing their ankles and took turns looking through Max's telescope.

"I don't want this day to ever end," said Dewey later. He was curled up next to Potter in front of the old stone fireplace. George had stoked the embers to life to ward off the evening chill.

Sara walked in carrying a huge bowl of popcorn. "Me, either, dearheart, and I think Potter feels the same."

"Potter thinks he's in heaven," said Max. He lowered his long body onto the couch. Jane was sitting at the other end. She was wearing a pink warm-up and had her legs tucked beneath her. Without conscious thought, Max lessened the space between them until his elbow rubbed the soft fleece of her pants.

George poured wine for the adults and gave Dewey a glass of soda with a cherry sitting on the bottom. They talked easily among themselves, slowly commenting on the day and the place and life. It was easy and relaxed, and Jane had almost fallen asleep, her head brushing the edge of Max's shoulder, when Dewey announced it was probably time to play a game.

"It's getting late, honey," Jane murmured. But Max had already flopped down onto the floor next to Dewey and Potter.

"How about a little Night Shadows?" he asked, and before Dewey could admit he'd never heard of that game, Max was directing him to turn out all the lights in the room except for one, a long goosenecked lamp that Max bent until a single beam of light shone on the far wall.

"Okay, sport," said Max, pulling Dewey down beside him. "Here goes..." And for nearly an hour Max taught Dewey how to twist his fingers and hands in front of the light to create animals and ghosts and monsters out of the shadows. Their creations cavorted cross the far white wall while Dewey's small body moved with delight. "I'll catch you," he shouted to Max, his fingers crossing until his shadow monster chased Max's through the beam of light.

Jane watched from behind them. The two figures were lost in their imaginary world. She didn't do that a lot with Dewey, she realized. In their carefully planned days fantasy slipped by them. It was too bad, she thought as Dewey's kneeling figure bounced on the soft carpet. Kids need fantasy, too. She'd have to remember that.

Dewey turned around. "You, try, Mom. Come on!" He edged over to make room for her.

Everyone decided Jane's shadows looked more like fuzzy eggs than animals, so Max took her hands in his larger ones and carefully curved her fingers until a perfect donkey pranced across the wide wall.

Dewey, Sara and George cheered her efforts, but Jane didn't hear much except Max's slow breathing on her neck. And the dance of the shadow donkey began to slow until Jane knew she'd better stop. It didn't seem like a child's game any longer, and she knew what her body was responding to was not a shadow. It was very real.

Jane bit down hard on her bottom lip and was grateful for the protective darkness behind the lamp. Lust, she thought. That is what was spread across her face like a scarlet letter. Here she was, in a roomful of people, and her body was going berserk. Efficient, dependable Jane Barnett was turning into a . . . a . . .

"Anyone for more wine?" Sara asked.

The lights went on, and everyone squinted into the glare.

"No, thanks," Jane managed, and then she turned toward Dewey. He had curled up on the braided rug in front of the fireplace, his head resting comfortably on Potter's furry back. "As for you, young man, it's way past your bedtime."

Dewey was watching her curiously. He pushed himself up. "Okay. You better go, too, Mom. You look funny."

"Funny?" Max said, looking Jane over. "I think your mother looks great."

Dewey squinted and examined her closely, then looked over at Max, his face serious. He shook his head wisely. "You don't know her like I do, Max," he said carefully.

George coughed to cover his laugh and lifted Dewey off the floor. He held him above his head until the serious expression on the round face turned to gleeful laughter.

Jane was standing now, and the height helped clear her head and steady her voice. She looked up at her giggling son. "I'm just tired, Dewey. Just like you." She smiled at Sara and George, then looked across at Max. "We've had a full day."

"Well, come back for a quick nightcap after you tuck in shadow man there," said Sara. "Such a marvelous day needs to be put to rest with a glass of George's finest brandy."

"It's tradition," George added. "You come back, Jane my girl, or we'll come in after you."

Five

—————

But when Jane returned to the living room a short while later, George, Sara and the brandy were absent.

"Hi," said Max. He stood looking out the window and into the darkened woods.

"Where is everyone?"

Max stayed where he was. "George wanted to check on something in the barn so Sara went with him."

Jane laughed uncomfortably. The lights in the room were dim and she couldn't see Max clearly.

Max watched her in the flickering light of the low fire. She still wore her pink warm-up and her hair was still pulled back in a ponytail, but tiny wisps of dark golden hair had escaped and curled around her face. Her high cheeks were flushed and her large green eyes glistened. She looked very young and very beautiful.

Max took a breath, held it for a minute, and then let it out slowly. "It's beautiful out there," he said at last, nodding toward the open windows. A cool breeze blew in, carrying with it the tang of aged evergreens and woodland flowers.

Jane nodded. She could hear the night sounds now, the birds settling down, the crickets calling and an animal howling somewhere far away. She walked over and stood beside him. "Such deep, beautiful sounds."

Max nodded. "Would you like to sit on the porch?" He spoke in a gentlemanly, almost courtly way that made Jane smile. Together, they walked through the French doors to a small screened-in porch off the back of the white house. There was an old wooden swing hanging from the ceiling that Sara had brightened with soft, colorful pillows. They made a soft, squishy sound when Max and Jane sat down.

"I always wanted one of these when I was a kid," Jane said. "But in the service you didn't invest in things that were difficult to move."

"Your father was in the military?"

Jane nodded. "For most of my childhood."

Max thought about that and about Jane as a youngster. About Jane playing. She'd lost that playful part of herself somewhere down the road. Or maybe it had been taken from her. He saw glimpses of it now and then, like today when along with Dewey and George they had made boats out of scraps of wood and raced them in the pond. She'd laughed fully when hers went bottom-up just off the shore. But laughter didn't come easily to her. He looked off into the darkness, acutely aware of her presence beside him, and he felt a strange kind of longing, a desire to be a part of that unknown past. "Did you like that?" he asked. "Moving all the time, I mean."

"Oh, I didn't mind then. It was all I knew. But I don't want that for Dewey."

"Why?" His feet were planted firmly on the floor, and with steady, easy pressure, he began to move the porch swing.

"Oh, many reasons. Because roots, ties, connections—these things are important. I want Dewey to have the kind of security that comes with that."

"Do you think your childhood wasn't secure?"

Jane didn't like people asking her personal questions. But Max spoke in a kind way that made her want to share. And there was something else, too. The sharing left a nice, warm feeling in its wake. "No," she said to Max, and then added quickly, "I mean *yes*, my life then was secure. But it was a different setup. I had two parents, a sister and brother. Dewey has only me."

Max looked sideways at her as she spoke, and in the soft shadow of the moonlight he could see the openness on her face. And the vulnerability was there too, stark and clear and startling. Sliding his arm up over the back of the swing, he leaned closer to hear. He dropped his hand lightly on her shoulder.

"Dewey's father isn't a part of his life," Jane said quietly.

"That's too bad. But Dewey is a happy little guy. You've done a good job, Jane."

Jane looked over at him and smiled. "Thank you. I've tried to do the right things for him. My parents retired in Hawaii so George and Sara fill in as a kind of extended family. They're great. Dewey loves them."

"I can tell. Does Dewey's dad live far away?"

"Yes."

"Is that hard on Dewey?"

Jane's heart twisted. No, it wasn't hard on Dewey. Because he couldn't remember having a father, thank God. Craig Barnett had gladly given up all rights to the son he bore years ago. And Jane knew he'd never go back on that. His own career and new life were far too important to him to ever acknowledge the two people whose lives he had almost ruined.

Max could feel the tightening of her shoulders beneath his hand. A slight shiver shook her body. "I didn't mean to push you into talking about this, Jane."

She twisted her head from side to side. "No, it's okay." Her voice was so soft that Max had to strain to hear her. He moved closer. "I'm just not used to it, that's all. I don't talk about it often. But no, it's not hard on Dewey. Craig was never a father in that sense. His contribution was purely biological."

Max sat quietly for a minute, thinking of his own childhood. He was sure he and his dad had had their ups and downs, but now, ten years after his father's death, all he remembered were the special times, such as the day his dad had taught him how to ride his bike and didn't seem to react when Max put a long scratch on the side of his dad's new Buick. He remembered how his dad had made him feel like a man at eighteen when together they had cried in the hospital lobby after Max's mother had given up her fight with cancer. And then the two of them had wrapped their arms across each other's shoulders and gone out to an all-night bar—a dimly-lit dive, he remembered—where they had drunk and talked and laughed and cried until the bartender's wife had finally driven them home to the little house on Harrison Avenue. There they had sat on the cold stone steps and watched the sun rise. He thought of his own dreams to be a father and how they had died in a single moment. A single, horrible moment. His fingers tightened across the narrow bone of Jane's shoulder.

"I've seen a lot," he said slowly, "but some things escape me, some things I can't begin to understand, like how a man can not want to raise his son."

Jane didn't answer. She leaned her head back until it rested on the curve of his arm. She closed her eyes and completely blocked out the thought of Craig Barnett not wanting to be a father.

"Do you hear that?" she asked. "I think it's a coyote."

Max strained his ears to catch the sound, but all he could hear was the wind whistling through the white pines. He wasn't at all sure Jane had heard anything, either, but he did know she didn't want to talk about Craig Barnett any longer. The man had hurt Jane in some way. And the thought of anyone inflicting pain on her caused a twisting in his gut that didn't belong in the deep peace of the night.

"I love it up here," Jane said a short while later. She moved her head slightly, and Max felt the brush of her hair against his cheek.

"Do you come here often?"

"Whenever we can talk Sara and George into bringing us."

"They're good friends—"

"Yes. Sara and I have been friends since high school. And when George came into her life, he had to accept me, too."

"That wouldn't have been hard to do." He began to massage her neck lightly and he could feel the muscles relax beneath his fingers.

Jane sighed. It was strange how easy the talk came and how nice his hands felt on her neck and shoulders. She could stay there forever, protected by the anonymity of the night.

"Jane, tomorrow when we leave here," Max was saying to her.

Leave here...leave this paradise... The thought made her enormously sad.

Max caressed the back of her neck and gently eased away the tension there. "...when we get back, I'm going to want to see you again. And it doesn't have anything to do with taxes."

Jane was still for a moment.

"Are you all right with that?" he continued to touch her lightly, but otherwise remained still.

"Max," Jane said, "I think I'd like to be friends, but—"

"I'm not talking friends, exactly, Jane. At first I thought I was. Not now."

Jane shifted on the seat, and it began to move again. The gentle movement was a welcome diversion. She breathed in the crisp night air and tried to pull her thoughts together. "In movies and books," she said slowly, "it's not talked about quite so matter-of-factly. Things happen if they're supposed to." She didn't want to talk about it, didn't want to tell him goodbye.

She paused and when she spoke again her voice was small and childlike. "Isn't that the way it is?"

"I don't know, Jane. Maybe I missed that movie."

"Maybe I missed it too. I don't seem to have the right comebacks."

"I'll give you some." Max shifted on the seat until he could look down into her moon-bright eyes. "Jane's comeback number one: 'Sure Max, what the hell. Let's see what happens.'" He ran one finger along the loose neckline of her sweatshirt and could feel the quiver of her body.

"Comeback number two," he said slowly. "'Nope, sorry. Get lost, Max. Bad idea.'"

Jane closed her eyes for a second. *Get lost, Max.* How could she tell him to get lost? Her body told her it might be too late for that, even while her mind was struggling fiercely to sort it all out.

"That last comeback is unsanctioned, by the way," Max said. "No backers." He dropped a kiss into her hair.

Jane looked up. "Is there a third?"

"Uh-huh. An old standby. Easy to remember and it worked for Valentino and Bogart, to name but a few." He lowered his head. And while the old wooden swing came to a stop, he closed the final space between them and kissed her slowly and deeply.

At first Jane was still, a quiet, willing recipient. The press of his lips to hers was welcomed by every inch of her body. She wanted it to go on forever, that one marvelous kiss. And then a wave of emotion burgeoned inside of her until she lifted her arms, circled his shoulders and held him there, pulling him closer to her and giving herself up to the passion and sweetness of his kiss.

When they broke apart to catch their breaths, Jane spoke. "You're right. It's effective. And easy to remember." Her voice was husky and her heart was banging against the wall of her chest. Max didn't seem to notice. He slipped his hand beneath the front edge of her sweatshirt, and Jane bit back the cry that leaped like a flame to her lips. One touch, one single touch and her soul was on fire.

His palm was cool against the heat of her bare skin, and she closed her eyes, soaking in the marvelous feeling and blocking out everything else.

Slowly he moved his hand across the flatness of her stomach, then higher up until his fingers curved over her breasts. Jane gasped. "Oh, Max..." she said. Her voice was ragged.

Max watched desire flit across her face and with his fingers he felt the need rise inside of her. Her passion was powerful, a raw and fierce need only thinly disguised by the lightness of her body. It was the wildness of it that made him stop and restrain his own building desire. At the same time he felt an insane need to protect her from anything she might be sorry for later. "Jane," he said softly, "it's been a while, hasn't it?"

Jane pressed her cheek into his chest.

"I don't want to push you too fast...."

Close to tears, she closed her eyes. "It's hard to explain, Max."

"Shh." he held her close and rocked her gently in his arms. "You don't have to explain."

Jane worked hard to keep from crying. He was so kind, she thought. Dear Max. He didn't know anything, but he understood in spite of that. Jane pressed herself more closely against his chest and clung to him, wrapping her fingers tightly around his arm. The desire, the passion that surged through her had been overwhelming, stunning her with its intensity. She had been caught on the crest of an enormous wave, and he had brought her down gently and safely.

She still wanted him terribly. That thought stunned her, as well.

For a while after Jane had left Craig, she had felt nothing sexual at all. Only a sick kind of numbness. But eventually feelings had come back, and the physical urges, as well. But none of that compared to the sweet, wild passion she felt in Max's arms.

The next day Jane and Dewey ended up riding back to Chicago in Max's Jeep because Potter had formed an attachment to Dewey that the six-year-old was reluctant to jeopardize.

"But we'll squash you, Max," Jane said.

"Great," Max answered, and he wrapped his arm around her to let her know closeness was not one of his hang ups.

The ride was bumpy and noisy and wonderful. Potter and Dewey sat happily in the small space in back and seemed to communicate with a language all their own.

Jane and Max sat up front and did the same.

Six

Dewey sat on the edge of the heated swimming pool, entranced. Beside him, sporting a wild pair of plaid swimming trunks, sat Uncle Leo.

"Hamburgers, Dewey, my friend," Leo was saying, "that's what started it all. You couldn't get a blasted burger worth your socks in the whole dagnabit town."

Uncle Leo grinned as he allowed Dewey time to imagine a burgerless universe, and then he plunged into an animated account of his progression from the owner of a small drive-in hamburger place on Cicero to the owner of an international chain that boasted Leo's grilled burgers in no fewer than fifty-seven countries. After years of the rat race, he had finally sold out to a conglomerate who gave him so much money for it, he had no idea how rich he was. Leo's Landing came soon after. A hobby, he told Dewey. Something to keep him out of trouble.

Dewey had already heard the story nearly a dozen times in the past few weeks, but it was always the first one he requested when Leo plopped down beside him and agreed to tell some tales. Jane had to admit that she enjoyed hearing the stories almost as much as Dewey did. Leo had become very special to her.

In those first few days after the trip to the farm, Jane had cautiously allowed Max to slip into her life. And Leo had been a wonderful part of the package.

One night Leo had invited her and Max to dinner at Leo's Landing, and it was then she got her first insight into Leo's crazy, marvelous career.

"After a while the money ceases to make sense, you know?" he had said. "So you got to reevaluate, figure it out, make it good again." Max had cut in then, telling Jane exactly how Leo had "made it good again." Leo had built a wing on a children's hospital, started a Wish Fund for terminally ill children and established a camp in New England for kids from the slums. "Leo likes kids," Max had added unnecessarily, and Jane's affection for the old man had deepened right along with the evening sky.

Jane watched Dewey now as he hung on to every word that came out of the old man's mouth. To Dewey, Uncle Leo was movie star, president, pope and a George Lucas character all wrapped up into one. And besides, since Leo and Max had come into their lives, his mom smiled more. He had realized soon on that the look he thought at first was kind of dopey, really meant she felt good about a lot of things, and after a few days Dewey decided he liked it—a lot.

"So, my small friend," Leo was saying now as he finished up his story, "there you have it in a nut-shell—Leo's looney life. Now that that's all clear as mud, how about if we put on some duds and trot on down to the garage. Got some cars down there that need polishing." He glanced over at Max and Jane. "We don't need your help. And Dewey and I are taking the Austin Healy out to dinner tonight. No room for you kids in that so you better make your own plans." He grabbed a towel and wrapped Dewey in it, then took him by the hand and the two went off to change.

Jane watched them go. He'd been doing that a lot lately—inviting them over to his sprawling estate, letting Dewey play with his collection of vintage automobiles or swim in the indoor pool or play pool in the recreation room. And he would carefully orchestrate events so Max and Jane were left alone as much as possible. Sometimes he'd include the Jennings, with whom he had felt an immediate kinship, and on those occasions, with two sets of matchmakers at work, Jane and Max didn't have a ghost of a chance.

Max's eyes, too, were following the unlikely cou-ple, the hunched old man and the small boy, as they walked through the sun room. "You know some-thing?" he said aloud. "Until you and Dewey came into Leo's life, he hardly ever used this place. He had been staying in the rooms above the restaurant."

Jane looked out the window at the rolling grounds, the stables and ponds and thick stands of giant oak trees that shaded the Lake County estate. She shook her head. "That's too bad. It's obvious he loves it out here. He's *alive* here."

"Now he is," Max said simply.

Jane shifted on the cushioned chaise. It wasn't just her relationship with Max that frightened her. Things were moving quickly, and although she and Dewey spent a lot of time discussing what good friends Max and Leo were, in Jane's heart she knew these friendships were becoming far more complicated than that. "Max," she said carefully, "Dewey loves Leo—"

"Sure. As it should be." He nudged her aside with his hip and sat next to her. "And Leo thinks Dewey hung the moon. That won't be disturbed, Janie. I think we both agree on that."

Jane shook her head against his shoulder and felt the sting of tears. "Of course," she said into the solid expanse of his chest. Half the time now Max read her thoughts and saved her the clumsy effort of explaining unexplainable fears. And each time he did he filled another hollow inside of her, and she wondered sometimes what would happen when he wasn't there anymore. Would she crumble? "Of course they will be there for each other."

Max wrapped her in his arms. He did that easily and often now, and Jane no longer froze. She allowed the intimacy of his embrace. But still he moved slowly, knowing with certainty that if he pushed too hard, Jane would move away from him. The thought of that brought immediate pain.

"Well, it looks like it's just the two of us for dinner. What'll it be?"

"Maybe I should be getting home." She bit her lip then, catching herself. "On second thought, there isn't a thing I have to do at home. And I'm starving."

"Good. I decided I'd better earn my license so I took on a new client. Tomorrow I start the job and I won't be as free as I've been."

"You mean on twenty-four-hour call?" Jane teased. "I was beginning to think this gumshoe stuff was all a hoax." It was true; Max seemed as free as the lake winds. In the middle of the day he'd show up at her house with excuses that defied responses. One day he'd come with his Jeep packed with geraniums. "Time to plant," he'd said, and had proceeded to fill her small garden with color. With the tax season behind her, Jane had been free, too. Maybe, Jane thought vaguely, once either of them got busy, the balloon would pop.

"Jane?" Max was watching her curiously. "I lost you there."

"Oh." Jane shook her head to scatter the thoughts. "Sorry. I was thinking about balloons."

"Now *there's* a subject." Max looked beneath the sea green surface of her eyes. "But not on an empty stomach. Want to go out?"

Jane looked down at her jeans, then back up at Max. "Do you mind if we just stay here? I'd like to get Dewey home as soon as he and Leo return. Tomorrow's a school day—"

Max was already standing. "That's a great idea. Come on, I just happen to be an expert at raiding refrigerators."

The kitchen was warm and spacious. Jane looked around at the huge skylights and the windows that invited the outdoors inside. She could see a slice of the lake from the wide window above the sink. A sprawling tile island filled the center of the room, and Max proceeded to fill it with most of the contents of Leo's stainless steel refrigerator.

Jane perched on a stool and watched him. "This is an unusual house for Leo," she said. "It's obviously designed for a family."

Max laughed. "Tell that to Leo. He'll agree one hundred per cent and then proceed to tell you how his nephew Max was letting it all go to waste."

"It's *your* house?"

"It's complicated. It's Leo's house really, but some years ago he put it in my name, badgered me for weeks to give him a dollar to legalize the so-called sale, and then spent the next few years telling me how wasteful I was, that I was crazy not to fill it with kids. I mean—" he feigned Leo's gravelly voice, "'—who would be so crazy to have a house like this and not fill it with happy kids—and maybe a wife thrown in besides?'"

Now it was Jane's turn to laugh. "So Leo has your life mapped out for you."

"Sort of." Max pulled a large tray from above the refrigerator.

"But you haven't filled the house. You don't even live here."

Max seemed to be concentrating on finding the right mustard. Finally he pulled it out and looked over at Jane. "No, I guess I've let Leo down."

"Why?"

"You mean why hasn't a thirty-six-year-old bachelor settled down?"

Jane nodded.

Max shrugged. "I've spent a lot of years coping with things that happen in spite of my efforts to keep life simple. You get in that rut and it's hard to move beyond it. You know what I mean?"

His voice had taken on a serious tone that Jane found disconcerting. This wasn't the carefree, handsome man who could lift her spirits with a smile. And she didn't know what he really meant. There seemed to be words left out of his explanation. She rested her elbows on the cool surface of the island and watched him carefully, her chin balanced in her hands.

Max looked up from the laden tray. "This ought to hold us for a while." He grinned, and the grave mood disappeared. "Come on Janie, I'll show you how to enjoy this refrigerator feast in style."

Jane took the basket of kaiser rolls he handed her and followed him out of the kitchen, through the dining room and into her favorite room. It was a family room that looked out over the swimming pool and treed yards that wound down to the lake. A stone fireplace dominated one wall, and wide French doors spanned another. A third was filled with built-in cabinets that stretched from floor to ceiling and were jammed full of books and records and tapes. Max set the heavy tray on the coffee table and pulled open one of the cabinets to expose the huge television set. "And here," Max said, "is a surprise. The world's largest collection of video tapes." Max rolled open a deep drawer and exposed hundreds of carefully labeled tapes. "Leo has everything, old television shows, new television shows, a thousand movies—you name it."

Jane shook her head. "And he probably never watches a one."

"Not often. But the kids, you see . . ."

Jane laughed and made herself comfortable on the rose-striped couch. It curved into an ell and looked big enough to seat ten. Her head fell back against the soft cushions. "This is unquestionably the grandest place on earth."

"Yeah, it's nice."

"Why don't you live out here with Leo?"

"Too far from work. Or at least that's what I tell myself."

"But the real reason, Max, is that you don't want to sink into this kind of domesticity."

"I suppose it's something like that. I guess deep down I agree with Leo—this house should be overflowing with kids and dogs." Max shoved a tape into the VCR and sat down next to her. "Hey, Janie, eat." He handed her a plate and began filling his own with thin slices of roast beef and turkey.

Jane sipped her wine and thought about the abrupt shifts in conversation. "Okay," she said. "But we haven't finished talking about this guy I know who obviously loves kids, has this wonderful house and hasn't married."

"I have. I mean I did marry once. A long time ago, over ten years now." He spoke quietly. "She—Elizabeth was her name—she died. We were married three months."

Jane heard the pain in his voice. It was an old pain that was still raw. She spoke quietly, "Max, I'm sorry. I didn't mean to pry."

"You're not prying, Jane. You share things like that with friends, people you trust." He focused his eyes on the flickering images playing across the television screen. In a few seconds the haunted look faded from his face.

On the screen an old television series was playing. It was vaguely familiar to Jane.

"This is *The Rockford Files*," Max said between bites of his enormous sandwich. His voice was less burdened now, filled with the charm Jane had grown used to. "Remember it? I figure it's as good a way as any to perfect my craft."

"Rockford..." Jane said. "Sure, he was a private eye, right?"

"Right. Only his life was filled with beautiful women and exotic trips to God-knows-where. He somehow escaped the humdrum following-errant-husbands kind of job."

"Is that what you do?"

"As seldom as possible. But I get some of it."

On the screen a curvacious blond was wrapping her arms around Rockford. "And my clients don't usually show gratitude that way," Max said. He laughed. "But every now and then...."

Jane narrowed her eyes. "Oh? So that's why you became a private investigator. The mystery clears." She poked him in the ribs with a stick of celery.

Max accepted the playful jab with pleasure. Each day Jane became more playful, less wary. He wasn't sure she was aware of it, but the subtle changes affected the way she looked and walked, the things she said. There was still a part of her that was inaccessible to him, but he hoped that soon that, too, might change.

Jane put the celery down and looked at Max thoughtfully. "I've seen you nearly every day for three weeks, Max," she said suddenly. The mood became more serious.

"We missed a day last Tuesday."

"Yes. And that day I missed you. One day, and I felt lonely not seeing you. I don't like missing you, Max."

"Easily solved." He wrapped an arm around her shoulders and pulled her close. Half of her sandwich fell onto his lap but Max ignored it. He kissed her gently. "We won't let Tuesdays happen. That will eliminate the problem."

"Max, that's not what I mean."

"I know." He lifted the hair off her neck and let it slide through his fingers. "But nothing's broken, Janie. Don't waste time trying to fix it."

Nothing's broken. No, not yet. But it might be. And it might be Max or it might be her.

As scared as the thought made her, Jane couldn't do a thing about it. Pushing him out of her life went against every single thing her heart was telling her. What would she say? *Goodbye Max, I don't ever want to see you again because I think I might be falling in love with you. And you know what that means. That means I'd have to trust you, Max, completely. And I don't . . . I don't think I can . . . so adios . . .*

"Jane, it's okay." Her body had become stiff, the set of her mouth tense, and he pressed her to his chest. "Hey, will you catch that Rockford?" he said, and as he gently held her frightened body, the two of them watched James Garner politely fend off a gorgeous redhead who insisted on paying her bill in the most interesting way.

Seven

"Saturdays are Dewey's, Max, Sorry." Jane wiped a single crumb from the table and dropped it into the wastebasket.

"Jane . . ." Max was trying to find the right words to explain the weekend to her. It was important and he didn't want to botch it. "Jane, I know you always spend the weekend with Dewey. But the Jennings have invited Leo to the farm and having Dewey along would mean a lot to all of them."

"We could all go."

"No, Jane. You and I aren't invited. Only Dewey."

"That's silly." Jane busied herself at the sink, carefully rinsing each plate before she put it into the dishwasher. They could hear Dewey playing a video game in the next room.

Max came up behind her. He wrapped his arms around her waist and breathed in the fresh smell of her hair. "Truth be known, Jane, I want to see what you look like away from Dewey. I'm crazy about the kid and I don't know if that's the only reason I hang around here, or if you can stand alone."

"When would we leave?"

"Anytime tomorrow. And we'll be back before Dewey gets home Sunday." Slowly he turned Jane around. With the sink at her back she had no place to go. Max cornered her there, his hands holding her shoulders gently. "Don't be afraid. It'll be a chance to see what this is all about, to just be together."

Jane took a deep breath, then met his eyes. Her heart was beating quickly.

"I know I'm not in a position to give advice on parenting, Jane, and it's obvious you do a great job. But letting Dewey go away for the weekend without you isn't all bad for him, either."

"I know. I know he needs to be independent of me sometimes—"

"And you of him," Max said softly.

Her gaze dropped, and she was silent for so long that Max thought he had angered her. But before he could speak, Dewey burst into the room.

"I won!" he squealed. "I captured the mushroom princess! Wanna see?"

His eyes were on Max, his chief competitor in the video game competition. Max stepped away from the sink and looked at Dewey in amazement. "You what?"

"Yeah, Max, it's the truth! Come on." He grabbed Max's hand and started to pull him from the room.

"Dewey," Jane said, and the tone in her voice froze his new tennis shoes to the floor.

"How would you like to go out to Sara and George's farm tomorrow?" She paused for just a second. "Without me, but Uncle Leo's going along."

"And Potter," Max added.

"Yeah!" Dewey's glasses slid down his nose when he jumped. He calmed himself for a minute and pulled his grin under control. "I mean, that's great that Uncle Leo and Potter are comin'. And I know they'll let you come another time, Mom. Don't feel bad."

Max looked from the small boy to his mother. And just before Dewey began tugging on him again to follow him, their eyes met. He saw a smile there. Small, a little frightened, but it was there nonetheless.

Max's cottage was a few hours from Chicago, a sunny ride along the southern curve of the lake and up the Michigan side. They stopped for lunch at a little inn near the sand dunes, and before leaving it Max went into the restaurant's small store and bought homemade biscuits, fresh strawberries and cream and a heaping basketful of what he told Jane were surprises for dinner. She had to be responsible all week he had said when she offered to help. This was his deal. So she had gone back and waited in the car, feeling pampered and spoiled and wonderful.

When they arrived at Max's place, Jane didn't see the house at first. It was hidden behind a thick stand of pine trees and bushes that Max had purposely left untended. They grew like a friendly wall between the road and his house. He drove slowly between the two brick posts marking the driveway and parked the Jeep in the narrow circle drive that passed the front door. "Here it is. What do you think?"

Jane stepped from the car. She viewed the width of the rustic, two-story cottage. "Max, I think it's perfect. It's a perfect Max house." She smiled, and together they walked up the three steps leading to the front door. Max ushered her inside.

Jane looked around and sighed. "Oh, Max, it really is wonderful."

He grinned and stayed close behind her as she walked across the clean pine floors to the other side of the house. The rooms were large and airy, filled with braided rugs and large, comfortable pieces of furniture, most of them purchased from craftsmen in the area. Oil paintings and framed photographs of the sand dunes and lake, chosen because someone simply liked them, accented the knotty pine walls. The back of the house was lined with windows and doors that opened out onto a spacious redwood deck. Standing there, Jane looked out over the white capped waters of Lake Michigan. She stepped outside and inhaled the scent of pine and lake and wildflowers. The scene was breathtaking.

"Between you and Leo, I'm going to be spoiled," she said softly. "This is so beautiful, Max."

"Well, it isn't fancy, but it's peaceful. We'll have to bring Dewey out here. Potter would love to have a friend to run the beach with."

"Yes," she murmured. Jane wrapped her fingers around the railing of the deck and looked out across the water. It was an unusually warm May day, and in the distance she could see several sailboats. Their brilliant orange and yellow and green-striped sails caught the wind and billowed majestically against the deep blue water. Dewey would love it here, and she loved it here. Except for the Jennings' farm, she hadn't taken Dewey away for weekends and vacations. She hadn't been able to afford it, so they had filled their free time with trips to parks and hiking in the woods behind the farm. They were wonderful times, but they weren't like this. They weren't filled with sailboats and antique cars. *They weren't filled with Max.*

That was the real difference. It was Max. He had come into their lives uninvited, and now he was there, as vital to their days as air and water. She shivered and wrapped her arms around herself.

"Cold? There's a bunch of windbreakers in the closet."

Jane shook her head. "Nope. It was just the view— it took my breath away."

"That I can handle. In fact, we need to get out there in the middle of those views. Come on." He pulled her inside. "We're wasting sunshine and fresh air. Put some shorts on and we'll hunt down crinoids and make you a necklace."

Jane had never heard of crinoids, but she didn't bother to ask about them. It didn't matter. The beach and Max were all she needed. She changed clothes in the small, pine-smelling bedroom Max led her to, then slid her overnight case into the closet. She looked around the room and silently thanked him for his sensitivity. The sleeping arrangements hadn't been discussed but Max had allowed her options.

When she returned to the deck Max was already there. His back was slightly bent, his hands on the railing as he gazed thoughtfully out over the lake. He was dressed in white jogging shorts and a red muscle shirt. It was the most Jane had seen of his body, and the sight stopped her in the doorway. His muscled shoulders were massive and the skin that stretched across them tan and smooth. Jane curled her fingers into a tight fist to restrain the desire to touch him. For a few minutes she stood there watching him, admiring him. She wondered what was going on in his mind. His face was only visible from the side, an awkward angle that allowed her a glimpse of his roughly chiseled nose, one cheekbone, his prominent chin. But what she saw she couldn't read. What did he see when he looked across the water? What were his hopes and dreams? There was much she didn't know about Max Harris.

"I feel a presence," he said without turning around.

"I've never been called a presence before," Jane said. She walked up beside him and leaned slightly against his arm.

"Well, that's what you are, my lovely Jane." Max moved his arm and welcomed her into its curve. "A presence to me."

She wore a thin gauzy top with a loose neckline, and his arm felt good against the exposed skin.

"I have to tell you, Jane, I feel pretty damn happy right now."

"It's that kind of a place, isn't it? I feel it, too."

"Oh, it's far from just the place, Jane."

She nodded, not needing to answer.

"The place helps," Max went on, "because it protects us from the other world. Fears and what have you."

Jane shifted in the circle of his arm. He'd done it again, known just how she was feeling.

Max caressed her arm. "But enough of that. Sometimes it's best not to analyze and just enjoy it. Like poetry."

"Yes," she said, her heart full. Her careful control slipped away so easily when she was with him. And Max was right. Today was for enjoying, not analyzing.

"There is one thing, though," Max said. "There's one thing you could do for me that would cap all this happiness." He looked down at Jane.

"Oh?" Jane felt a flush beneath the thin material of her blouse. *No, Max,* she pleaded silently. *I don't think I'm ready...*

"Yeah." Max said. "The highlight will be seeing you with that gorgeous head of hair loose and free as God intended."

Jane felt a rush of relief. She felt almost giddy. She fingered the thick ponytail and forced her rapid heartbeat to slow. All he wanted from her was for her to let her hair down. Funny. She had almost done it today when she'd changed clothes. And then at the last minute she had brushed it back again and slipped a band around it. It had been a long time since she had let her hair blow in the breeze, free and easy. Years ago she had discovered that tightly bound hair was far safer when Craig raged. And afterward the habit of buns and rolls and ponytails was too ingrained to break easily. Strange, she thought, how her past still bound her in these thin, odd ways.

"Later maybe," Max said as he watched the conflicting emotions flit across Jane's face.

She smiled up at him. "Maybe. But don't we have a date with a crying node now?"

Max laughed. "Crinoid. Fossils. Tiny little animals that lived in the water long before you were around. Even before *I* was around." Max lowered his head and spoke gravely into her ear. "I can see, Ms. Barnett, that you have a lot to learn about our mighty lake here."

"But I'm a willing student."

"Okay, you've got yourself a professor. Let's go."

They walked single file down the narrow stone path to the beach, Jane following carefully in Max's footsteps until they reached the level stretch of sand and stones. The beach stretched north as far as she could see. It was nearly deserted.

"Where is everyone?" Jane asked. She slipped out of her canvas shoes and set them on a large rock.

"It's still early in the season. And this warm weather is an oddity. I've been here in May when you could still see your breath in the air." Max stooped and examined the sand. "Aha!" he said suddenly. "Janie, you're good luck. Here it is, your first crinoid. And it's a perfect lily."

Jane moved to his side and stared down into his open palm. A small, lily-shaped shell the size of a shirt button rested there.

"Sometimes they're broken, but this is perfect. And see the tiny hole?" He pointed to the edge of the shell. "That's to string it on a necklace for you."

"It's beautiful." Jane took the fossil from him and held it up to the sunlight. Such a small thing, and so perfect for this day. She wrapped her fingers around it and held it tightly. "I love it, Max. Thank you."

He looped an arm around her waist. "It's just the beginning." They walked on down the beach, arm in arm, stepping into the shallow end of the cold waves, then burying their toes in the sand to warm them before continuing. They walked and ran and stopped to search for crinoids in shallow pools carved by the tide.

It was a perfect afternoon. When the sun started to set Jane grew pensive.

"What's the matter, Janie?" Max asked. They were sitting together at the end of a dock in front of Max's cottage. It swayed lightly with the crash of waves against its steel supports.

"I don't want this time to end. It's been such a perfect day."

"Well, it won't end. Not yet anyway. I am going to fix you a dinner to die for."

"And the man cooks, too." Jane snuggled into his side. "Such a deal. I haven't felt this relaxed in a long time, Max."

"I guessed that," he said, playing with the damp ends of her ponytail. "It becomes you, Jane."

His voice had grown suddenly husky. It had happened on and off all afternoon. A word, a gesture, the rub of their damp cool skin together. They hadn't talked about it, but the sexual tension had flourished between them until Max would have to tell a joke, or Jane would be overcome by the need to find another crinoid.

"Max," Jane said slowly, moving her fingers over the rough edge of the dock, "these past weeks with you have meant a lot to me. I can't always express myself the way I want to, but I do want you to know how much you mean to me—"

"You express yourself just fine, Jane." Max felt unbridled flames find his desire in the cruelest way. He didn't know how much longer he could hold his love for her in check.

There were times, like this afternoon, when he could feel Jane reaching out for him, could feel her trying to let herself trust him completely. It caused him pain, because he didn't know how to help her. Jane loved him. He knew it, even if she didn't. It was in her eyes and her voice and her touch, and was as real to him as the churning water at their feet.

"Look," he said softly, and pointed to the horizon. Where land met water, the color was deepening. It was no longer the peaceful blue of the afternoon, but appeared nearly black, and above them the sky was filled with enormous dark gray clouds. "There's a storm coming—an early summer storm coming out of the blue."

"I don't want a storm to end this perfect day," she said quietly.

"It'll be beautiful. You'll see. We'll eat and then watch it together. Trust me, Janie...."

While Jane showered and changed into jeans and a sweatshirt, Max got in his daily run. Jane was on the deck, lighting the charcoal grill when he returned. He was breathless and his body was covered with a wet sheen from the exercise. His thin shirt clung to his shoulders and chest, and Jane swallowed hard to cover the emotion that consumed her. It came on as strong as the powerful waves beating hard now against the shoreline. Her feeble effort to tame the sensations failed miserably.

Max came up beside her. "I'd hug you crazy but you'd end up soaking wet. You look great standing there at the grill. Just great." Max paused for gulps of air.

Jane concentrated on sticking the match into the coals and avoiding the wind. "I should run. I don't exercise much."

"You should try it. We could run together. I'd teach you the ins and outs." He walked through the screen door as he talked and returned in a minute with two cold beers. He handed one to Jane.

"Run together? That's a great idea, Max. You could run on out to my place—it'd only take you an hour or so—and then we could amble around a block or two."

Startled, Max realized that that was not what he had intended. What he had meant was that when they were living together, when they were *married*, they could roll out of bed and hit the jogging path—together.

And the fact that he fully intended to marry Jane Barnett gave him great pleasure.

"What's so funny, Max," Jane said. "You look like the cat that swallowed the canary, maybe a whole truckload of canaries."

Max couldn't get rid of the grin. He felt terrific! "Nothing's funny. Everything's just great!" He kissed her then, trying to hold back his chest to keep Jane free of his wet shirt. "There. That says it all."

Jane looked at him curiously. "You're crazy, Max, do you know that?"

"I know all sorts of things. And right now, while you sit, look beautiful and watch that purply sky, I'm going to shower and then wine and dine you." And then, well, then what would be would be, he thought to himself. There wasn't any hurry; Jane was worth waiting for.

By the time they'd eaten the fresh, grilled salmon with dill sauce and Max's baked potatoes, crispy on the outside and flaky inside with melted cheese, Jane didn't think she'd ever move again. "But the strawberries and cream," Max reminded her. "And there's homemade shortbread."

"Oh, Max, have mercy," she groaned.

"All right, mercy it is." He stood and filled a plastic sack with the remains of their meal, collected the plates and silverware and deposited them in the sink, then handed Jane a jacket. "We'll walk off some of this, then come back for dessert."

Jane glanced outside. "Max, it's going to pour soon."

"I know. So we'd better get a move on. I'm going to introduce you to our first summer storm. Jane, they're beautiful. I think you'll like it. Storms out here are different from anywhere else."

Jane walked through the door reluctantly. Curling up in front of the fire with Max at her side had much more appeal. "You're sure we want to do this?"

Max nodded and flicked a switch that threw beams of light across the back terrace and on down the stone steps to the beach. "We won't stay out long."

A strong gust of wind, brisk but not cold, pushed them back against the door for a brief second as they stepped outside. Jane's hair tugged against the scarf that held it in place. Carefully, with one hand tucked into Max's belt, she followed him down the steps.

As they reached the beach the roar of the waves increased. Max spoke into her ear so she could hear him. "Don't worry, Jane. I won't let go of you." He wrapped an arm around her waist, and Jane melted into the warm, protective curve of his body. Together they lowered their heads into the wind and headed toward the dimly lit dock.

Jane stepped onto it uneasily. "Are you sure we can't greet the storm from here?"

"It'd never hear us," Max said.

"Oh, I don't know." Jane wiped at the fine spray of water that had collected on her cheeks. "I can be real loud when I put my mind to it."

Max chuckled into her hair. "I'll protect you, I promise." He pulled her even closer, and the two walked carefully down the weaving pier. Below, the choppy water slapped loudly against the sides.

The sky, an endless mass of deep, murky blackness, seemed touchable. Along the coast tiny lights shone in the distance, giving evidence to houses hidden in the trees. Everything that was visible—a few boats moored to neighboring piers, the trees and twinkling lights—moved wildly back and forth, pushed by the powerful winds that seemed to come from several different directions at once.

"See out there, Jane?" Max stood apart from her for a moment while he pointed into the distance. "A freighter, probably carrying grain."

"With a seasick crew, I'd bet." Jane watched the lights of the vessel dip, disappear, then flicker again.

There truly was a beauty to it all. The moving blackness and wind-tossed lights, the vessel in the middle of the churning great lake. The water and sky seemed to fuse into one living, majestic mass.

Power, she thought. That's what was so overwhelming about it. And here she and Max were, insignificant specks in the midst of it. "It's majestic, Max," she said softly. "Bigger than life, and certainly us."

Beside her, Max nodded. "And it's never the same. I think that's what I like most. It's always exciting because it's always new—"

A strong wind from the north blew away the end of his sentence, and Jane swayed slightly away from him. Before Max could pick up his thought, another more powerful gust caught Jane and heaved her light body to the edge of the dock.

Her arms swung crazily in the air. Before she could scream, Max grabbed her firmly and pulled her back until she was pressed tightly into his chest.

Beneath his hands her body shook. "Hey, Janie," he said, the words spoken so softly she could barely hear him. "I'm sorry..."

Jane shook her head to let him know she was fine, but her body refused to calm itself.

"No," Max said, his voice full of regret. "You're not okay. I shouldn't have let go. I'm so sorry."

The wind was whipping wildly about them now, and he turned toward shore, holding her tightly to his side.

"I'd make a terrible sailor," she whispered.

"I think you're great. I just need to pick my storms more carefully. This one isn't very hospitable."

"But there is a beauty to it," Jane said, her fear beginning to fade with the press of his body. "Awesome, as Dewey says."

A huge wave crashed against the pier as she spoke, and the cold water came down like a waterfall on top of both of them. Their yelps sounded above the roar of the wind as they jumped quickly to the safety of shore.

"Oh, Max," Jane said, turning to stare at him. He was drenched. "Look at the two of us." A small giggle bubbled from her throat, and before she knew it she was clinging to him, tears from her laughter mingling with the lake water.

Max lowered his head until his lips touched her wet hair. "When I show my woman a storm, I don't do it halfway." He wrapped his arm around her waist.

"Come on, let's get out of this mess. King Neptune rescuing Venus, here we go...."

Jane looped her arm around his back, and they lowered their heads against the wind, running crazily toward the cabin steps. Ahead they could see the welcoming lights of the cabin. Behind them the roar of the storm continued, growing louder until Jane could feel it pounding inside of her.

"Now see," Max shouted, "wasn't this f—"

But his words were a second too late and the cabin was several yards too far away. At that moment the storm broke and it began to pour, suddenly, wildly, furiously. In shocked surprise, Max and Jane were frozen in their steps.

"I don't think," Max said carefully, "that this was one of my better ideas, Jane."

And then he grabbed her and they ran the remaining few steps, their laughter fueling them as the rain beat mercilessly at their backs.

They stood in the shadowy light of the cabin as water collected in pools at their feet. "You look beautiful, my rain-drenched Jane," Max said.

"Well, at least I don't melt." She turned her face up toward his. "Do you perchance have a towel?"

In wet tennis shoes, Max trod through the house and in seconds he returned with large beach towels and wrapped Jane in one. "You also need a kiss, a shower, a drink and a fire."

"In that order?"

"The fire and drink are up for grabs."

"That's all?" She hadn't moved. Her head was tilted back. Rain-darkened curls were matted against her cheeks and forehead, but Jane didn't notice. All she noticed was the sudden heat and Max's slightly parted lips.

Max didn't answer her. His arms were still around her drenched body, and with easy grace he lifted her off the ground and kissed her, a kiss that was long and slow and full of joy.

When he returned her to the ground Jane had forgotten about the shower, but Max slowly led her back to the small bedroom. And then before the intensity of the moment ran away with him, he stepped back out into the hallway and softly closed the door behind her.

When she returned a short while later Max was kneeling in front of the fire, adjusting the logs with an iron poker. He'd dried himself off and changed into a sweatshirt and pants.

Jane walked quietly over to him. She'd wrapped herself in the warmest thing she had brought along, a thick terry cloth robe that reached almost to the floor.

When Max felt her presence and looked up, a huge lump formed in his throat, and for a second he couldn't speak.

Her hair was loose and hung in waves about her shoulders, and the firelight was reflected in its thick strands. She smiled at him. "Are the drink and the fire still on our agenda?"

The clean, soapy smell of her reached his nostrils. Behind him the fire heated his back. Max hardly trusted himself to stand. But he did, and while Jane curled up on the couch in front of the enormous fire, Max walked over to the bar and poured them each a snifter of brandy and steadied himself with deep breaths of cool air.

Before returning, he fiddled with the stereo until he heard the easy strains of big band music. He wasn't sure what it was—Benny Goodman or one of the other greats—but it seemed perfect for the moment, so he turned it up and then walked back across the room. Jane was cushioned against the tall back of the couch, her eyes closed and a soft smile on her face.

He sat down carefully, not sure she wasn't asleep.

"Kiss, shower, fire…it's time for the brandy," she said softly, and opened her eyes halfway.

Max handed her the snifter, then took his own. "Here's to storms," he said. He held his glass out to hers.

Jane tapped it lightly, and the ring of the crystal sounded in the fire-heated air. "And to one of the nicest days of my life."

Max nodded. "That, too." They sipped their drinks in easy silence. When Max refilled her glass, Jane accepted it with a smile. The fire, the brandy, the day— she wanted to hold on to every second of it. When Max began gently rubbing her shoulder, the moment seemed all the more perfect. She would remember for always the slide of the robe across her shoulder, the heat of his fingertips on her skin.

She sipped her drink and closed her eyes. The fine, comforting sounds of the music surrounded her. Her head felt light, and her senses reeled with the clean musky scent of Max beside her. And somewhere not too far away was the storm, its violence churning the lake and charging the air. She gave in to all the sensations, warm and cold, sweet and strong, and let the brandy relax her until it all seemed like a dream, a wonderful dream she wanted to be a part of for a long, long time.

"Jane..."

Her name registered as an intrusion in the lovely, sensuous world. For a minute, she blocked it out.

"Jane..." Max said again. He had moved closer, and had slipped his arm around her to flatten it against her back.

Jane struggled to open her eyes and found Max's face only inches from hers. His features shifted slowly into focus, and all the lovely sensuous images that had drawn her to this man. His eyes, a deep, clear, navy blue, held her.

"Jane," he said gently, "I love you."

She didn't move.

"I've loved you for a while now," Max continued. His voice was low and firm, filled with the gentleness that Jane had come to love. "I can't really remember when it began. But it did, and you've become a part of me." He brushed a strand of hair from her cheek. "Jane," he said, "I want to make love to you."

Jane felt the sting of tears.

Max stroked her cheek. "I don't want to scare you or frighten you, I only want to love you."

Jane moved her head against the sofa. Her hair fell over his hand, and she kissed the edge of his finger when he caressed her mouth. "Max, I love you, too," she whispered.

"It's not so awful is it?"

"It's complicated."

"So's life, Janie. You deal with it." He held her in his arms now and he could feel her heartbeat against his chest. She clung to him.

Max kissed her hair. "It's been a long time for you."

"A lifetime," she said, and she felt the tears well up again.

Max kissed the soft skin of her neck. She was still quivering. "Jane, you know I'd never hurt you, don't you?"

She nodded against his chest. "I don't think you would."

Gently he slipped his hand into the fold of her robe and sought her breast. He felt Jane's sharp intake of breath as he circled it, then cupped it in the curve of his hand and gently massaged it. "May I open this?" He tugged at the sash of her robe with his other hand.

Jane was silent.

Max slowly loosened the sash and pushed the robe apart until her bare skin was lit by the flames of the fire. He dipped his head low and began licking the round hardness of her breasts.

Jane's heartbeat was irregular. She plunged her hands into Max's thick hair, then gasped at the bolts of pleasure pulsing through her as he rubbed her stomach, then slid his fingers across her abdomen and lower.

With a low moan, she stiffened.

Max stopped and pulled slightly apart. In the thin light of the low fire he could make out the fear that marred her face.

She squinched her eyes shut and fought for air.

"Jane," he said softly, "It's okay. I'm going too fast."

"No—"

"Then what?"

"I . . ." Tears choked her voice. She wanted him so badly. She wanted *this*, for God's sake. She wanted Max, wanted him to be a part of her. Maybe she wanted it too badly, she told herself, and with that thought silent tremors passed through her body like aftershocks.

"Just tell me, Jane."

"I can't."

"Yes, you can." He held her face between his palms. "You can tell me, because I love you. I won't hurt you."

The tears she had held back so valiantly began to fall. They came in sheets like the rain outside the windows. Max kissed them away, but held her there next to him, waiting, loving her.

Jane's voice was ragged when she spoke again, torn with tears and memories. But she spoke clearly and her wet eyes were fixed on Max's face.

"He hurt me, Max," she said. "Craig Barnett hit me, he broke my arms, he blackened my eyes and he turned me into nothing." The words hung in the still air between them.

Before Max could begin to understand such a hellish reality, Jane continued. "And maybe the worst thing of all, Max, the thing that is hardest to live with, is that he left me with a thousand demons to fight." Her voice dropped to a thin whisper. "And I don't know how to get rid of them."

Eight

Max didn't move.

He sat in silence, holding her while the horror of five years of her life shook her body like a volcanic eruption. He listened while she talked of hair being pulled, of summers spent in long-sleeved dresses to hide the purple shame of her husband's rage, of self-blame for another's irrational behavior, of self-doubt, of self-loathing. In his mind he pictured Jane crouching in a locked closet with a tiny infant in her arms, of her final flight down a rain-muddied alley in the middle of the night, through unfamiliar streets, until at last she reached the shelter that may have saved two lives.

"One life," she said softly. "One life was all that mattered. Dewey's."

While he listened, Max tried to distance himself from her story because he knew if he couldn't put some space between himself and Jane's horror, he would be of little help to her tonight. He knew if he let himself absorb everything, his own rage would smother him and he'd be useless. So calmly, carefully, he rationally analyzed the irrational atrocities of Jane's life. He listened, and in his mind he carefully recorded the story of a life that had been stripped of hope and trust and filled instead with a crushing fear. And that awful fear lingered still, Max now knew, in this gentle woman with whom he'd fallen totally and passionately in love.

"My darling Jane," was all he said as he held her tightly, stroking her hair and rocking her gently back and forth. "My beautiful love..."

Hours later when he felt her body finally relax and the tears had dried on her cheeks, he lifted her exhausted form in his arms and carried her, sleeping, into his bedroom. For a while he sat beside her on his wide, safe bed, not wanting to leave her alone even in sleep. Finally he kissed her softly on the lips, and walked quietly from the room.

It was the silence that awakened her, she thought later. The crashing waves and relentless rain had stopped, leaving an enormous silence that pulled her from a deep, dreamless sleep. She lay still for a long time.

She had vowed long ago not to pull anyone else into the absurdity of her life with Craig Barnett. Sharing it gave it a substance, she wanted it denied, so she had refused to talk about it. Until last night. Now, hours later, she felt completely drained—and curiously light. In the midst of the excruciating pain of retelling her past, something good had happened. She could sense it, but not yet name it.

Jane lifted herself on one elbow and tried to focus on the room. It wasn't the small bedroom in which she'd changed clothes. She was alone in Max's bedroom, the spacious masculine haven that filled one side of the upstairs. Through the east windows she could see a thin light filtering across the horizon. It was nearly daybreak. The cabin was silent.

Slowly she swung her legs over the side of the bed. The movement made her head ache, and when she pressed her fingers to her face, she felt the puffy skin, a reminder of her tears. Max had taken on her burden last night. It was certainly more than he had bargained for those weeks before when he'd sat across her desk and unnerved her with his searching blue eyes. She wondered briefly if he regretted opening this part of her life. What was he to do with it now that he had it?

Steadying herself on her feet she tightened the sash of her robe and made her way down the cold staircase.

Memories of another predawn trip to the kitchen to get a glass of warm milk flitted across her mind as she fumbled for the light.

She had just met Max. And even then he had managed to invade her heart. And now he had invaded her horror, as well.

She could still feel his arms around her as he had let her speak. They were strong and gentle, giving her security and comfort at once. Her dear Max. Max, who loved her. The thought was still too new to register completely, but he had said it, said he loved her, and when she had looked into the honest blueness of his eyes, she had known there was no doubt about his sincerity. Max didn't give love easily and carelessly, and it hadn't been a small protestation for him. It was as real as the sunrise. She wanted to touch that love, to caress it and press it to her. Mostly she wanted to return it.

But Jane knew above all else that wanting to love Max and actually loving him were two completely different things.

A small noise made her lift her head. She looked through the window out onto the deck. As her eyes adjusted to the changing light of dawn, she made out a figure sitting near the rail. It was Max, sitting in the same navy warm-up he'd had on last night. His back was curved, bent over like an old man's, and his elbows rested on his knees, his forehead pressed into the knuckles of his hands.

Jane walked silently through the kitchen door. He didn't move, didn't seem to hear her as she padded softly across the redwood planks. As she grew closer the sound became more distinct.

She stopped then. Now she understood as she watched the shaking of his shoulders, and she now knew what Max was doing with the horrible burden of her past.

Her heart clattered noisily in her chest, and she fought the tears pressing against her lids. She wrapped her hands around herself and tried to still her own trembling, but her eyes stayed on Max.

In the silent, ragged way of male grief, Max was weeping for her pain.

Although the weekend had been a turning point, neither Jane nor Max acknowledged it with words. A high wall had been torn down, leaving only scattered traces of itself and both Jane and Max accepted its disappearance silently. In their separate, private ways they dealt with the pieces that were left.

Jane knew Max's gentleness was deeper, his patience greater, because of what he'd learned. Sometimes his kindness overwhelmed her so that she thought her heart might burst with love for him. At other times she felt weak, incapable of giving Max the complete trust he so fully deserved. But all the time she loved him. Of that Jane was certain.

They moved into the early, lazy days of summer carefully. Jane wanted to stop time, to bask in Max's love, to let it fill her so completely that there wouldn't be room for doubts and fears and demons.

Instead Max filled the days to the brim and time moved swiftly on.

"Max, let's go sailing," Dewey shouted one Saturday morning. Nearly every weekend was spent together—Max, Dewey and Jane—and they were often joined by the Jennings and Leo, as well.

"Sailing it is, sport," Max said. "But let's make it a men's day. Your mom and Sara mentioned something horrible sounding. 'Shopping' I think."

"Argh," groaned Dewey, grasping his throat.

"That's what I thought, too," said Max. He laughed, grabbed Dewey by the waist and threw him into the air, catching him just in time to save his third pair of glasses in a month from biting the dust.

Leo and George came along, and the four-man crew pushed the twenty-foot sloop away from the private slip just east of Lake Shore Drive. Dewey's blond hair blew like crazy in the breeze, and Max watched as the childish laughter rang out on the lake breeze. He was a neat kid. A great kid. *His* kid, or at least that's how he was beginning to think about him. He knew that wasn't right, that he had to watch those ties or there was a chance Dewey could be hurt. Max would rather die than have that happen. But it was damn hard to hold back with a kid like Dewey. They were already kindred spirits.

He wasn't sure where things stood with Jane. Max wasn't a patient man by nature, but he knew with this relationship he had to be. And he also knew his patience and love might not be enough. Only Jane could break down the barriers and allow herself to trust a man completely. He had done about all he could do.

"Hey, Max, look at me!"

Max glanced up to see the jiggling boy balancing on a metal food box Leo had brought along from the restaurant. Both of Dewey's small hands were waving gaily in the wind and his eyes were closed behind his glasses, blocking out the sea spray.

"Dewey," Max yelled. "Get down from there!"

The urgency in his voice caused Dewey's eyes to open wide and his hands to stop their balancing act. And it was then that a huge wave slapped up against the side of the boat. The boat lurched, and the small body tumbled over the side and into the white-capped water.

Max didn't stop to think. In a fraction of a second he was overboard, slicing through the icy water, and coming up beside the frightened, thrashing child whose life jacket kept his head above the water.

Dewey threw his short arms around Max's neck, clutching frantically. In three long strokes Max was back at the boat and he and Dewey were being hoisted up over the side. Leo, his features lined with fear, was there with thick blankets.

Max wouldn't let Dewey go. He held him close, pressed against his chest until he heard soft whimperings from the child.

"It's okay, Dewey," he said, pushing him slightly away so he could check his color.

"I'm sorry," Dewey whispered.

"You ought to be," Max said, trying for a light tone. Slowly Max forced his heart to beat regularly. He masked the terror he had felt behind a small smile. "Guess what, sport?"

Dewey looked up into Max's face and squinted against the sunlight. "What?"

"Tony the tuna just inherited a new pair of specs."

Dewey reached automatically for his glasses. They were gone. "Oh, damn!"

The terrible tension of the accident was released in the small boy's unlikely outburst, and Max, Leo and George tried to hide their relieved grins.

"My mom'll kill me, Max!"

"We'll figure it out," Max said, tousling the boy's damp hair. No, she wouldn't kill him. Nothing much mattered in light of his safety. The fear that had paralyzed Max for that single excruciating moment when Dewey had swayed had thrown Max back ten years to the darkest day of his life. And when Dewey had surfaced safely, it was a gift from the gods. He was safe; that was all that mattered.

And that was the weighty thought that Max carried around with him the rest of the sun-drenched day. Nothing much mattered but Jane and Dewey. Their safety, their lives. He had thought Elizabeth's death had rendered him unable to love with his whole body and soul, unable to bear the responsibility for another human. But Jane had changed it all. She was his life now. She and this freckle-faced kid for whom he'd lay down his life.

"Okay, Dewey," Jane said that evening when the sailors made their weary way home. She stood at the door with her hands on her hips. "Where are they?"

Max stood behind his charge, his face impassive.

"Where's what, Mom?" Dewey asked innocently.

"Your glasses, that's what. Dewey if you—"

"Oh, that!" Dewey said. "Yeah, the glasses."

"We didn't like the style," Max cut in. "Too brainy looking."

"Yeah, Mom. Too brainy," echoed Dewey.

"So we got some new ones," Max said. "They're—"

"Cool," Dewey inserted.

"Yeah," said Max. "They're real cool. The optometrist over on Wabash is doing a rush job. We'll have them Monday."

Jane frowned, her eyes darting back and forth between the two males. They were keeping something from her. And Max, she suspected, was protecting Dewey from a mother's worry and displeasure. Like a good father would do, she thought with a start.

Max grinned then, and Dewey turned around and gave him an enormous wink.

Sudden tears sprang to Jane's eyes, and she spun around and opened the coat closet to hide them. She grabbed a sweater from a hook and mumbled to Dewey and Max, "Since I seem to have missed out on all the fun today, I think the least you two guys can do is take me out for frozen yogurt."

Max and Dewey quickly agreed.

A week later Jane made up her mind. Her decision was right and good, she thought as she headed for the phone—and had been surprisingly easy to make. *Everything* seemed right and good somehow and gloriously, joyously wonderful.

"Max," she said without preamble when he picked up the phone, "I'd like you to come here for dinner tonight. Dewey is spending the night with a friend, so it'll be just the two of us. Just you, me and my market's finest."

She kept her voice gracious and warm but never let on about the seduction she had planned. She smiled secretively into the phone receiver. She'd make it a wonderful night. A perfect night. A night that only two people who loved one another as she and Max did were entitled to.

Through the weeks and days and hours spent with Max, her love for him had unraveled until she finally felt there was nothing holding it back. It was bigger than either of them separately and as open to life as tulips in the spring.

They hadn't talked about marriage, and she suspected it was only Max's profound patience that had kept them off that topic. He didn't know where she stood because she hadn't been able to tell him. She hadn't been able to show him. But she was ready now.

What was that saying? Jane thought as she knelt before her flower bed, cutting golden daisies and baby's breath for the table. *This is the first day of the rest of your life.* She had always thought it silly and trite. Tonight it felt right.

Max had said he'd be there at seven, and Jane worked feverishly all afternoon making everything perfect. Finally, an hour before his arrival, she stood back and surveyed her hard work. The house was clean and shining, filled with the fresh scent of flowers from her garden. She had pushed the small gateleg table over in front of the garden door and draped it with a linen cloth. Her mother's silver gleamed next to the crystal wineglasses. Okay, she thought, everything's ready. The champagne was chilling in the refrigerator, the lamb was marinating in a fragrant bath of fresh herbs and the pie was in the oven. She cut off the tip of the tapered candles so they'd light more easily, straightened a linen napkin and decided she had just enough time to soak the day's work out of her limbs and to get dressed. And then Max would be at her doorstep.

The thought of him had her singing as she made her way to the tub.

At seven Jane was ready. Taupe linen slacks and a silk blouse felt smooth and sensuous on her bathed and powdered body. She couldn't remember ever pampering herself this way before, but tonight it somehow was right. It was a night for pampering. Her dark blond hair fell loose and free around her shoulders. She felt sexy and she felt in love.

She checked the clock. Seven-ten. Jane frowned, then walked over to the phone and called the number for time and weather. Dewey had probably been fiddling with the clocks again, taking them apart, with Max's enthusiastic encouragement, and figuring out how they worked. Usually they didn't after he got done.

The phone message confirmed the time. Traffic, she thought. He had probably run into a mess on the Dan Ryan. Ten minutes wasn't much anyway. Except Max wasn't usually late. Well, she thought, love was making her act in peculiar ways . . . so maybe it was making Max lose track of time.

She walked slowly into the kitchen and checked the meat and the rice pilaf. Everything smelled wonderful. She would just put it all on hold. It'd be fine. Max would be there soon.

She sat on the small floral sofa in front of the window that looked out onto the street. A magazine sat open on her lap, but her thoughts were scattered as she waited for the first glimpse of his car as it turned onto Greendale Lane. Love was a miracle, she thought. Everything looked different, felt different—the clouds, the color of the sky, the taste of food.

At eight-fifteen, Jane dialed Max's number.

The familiar voice on the answering machine made her smile. And since he wasn't there he must be on his way; no need to worry. Just a slight delay somewhere along the way. Probably a client, she thought, and walked into the kitchen to reheat the meat.

At eight-thirty she lit the candles on the table, and at nine she blew them out, staring through damp eyes and the rim of her empty wineglass at the puddle of wax on the linen tablecloth.

She sat alone at the table, seeing nothing, her heart tossing and turning on a sea of anxiousness and disappointment. He wasn't coming. She'd tried his patience far too long—she knew that. Max had been gentle and kind; he had loved her with kid gloves, getting only as close as he thought she could handle. She knew how hard it had been for him sometimes; she had heard it in sharp intakes of breath, had seen the sheen he'd wipe from his forehead after a long, tender kiss. She was pushing him to the limit. But she hadn't been able to help it; she thought he had understood.

And now he wasn't coming. Tonight of all nights, he wasn't coming.

Jane turned the record off and dialed his number one more time. She hung up before the message was finished. She didn't want a recording of Max's voice; she couldn't make love to that. She wanted Max.

As the wine-induced haze began to clear, her thoughts fell back into neat patterns and she began to worry even more. How selfish she was being, thinking only of her disappointment. What if... what if something happened? Her mind began to race. By nine-thirty Jane was nearly frantic. Her mind was ravaged with grisly images of accidents, robberies, violence. No, she thought, trying desperately to calm herself. She knew that if anything bad had happened, Leo would know. And he would have called her directly. Leo! Maybe Leo knew why Max hadn't come....

Jane rushed to the phone and fumbled with her telephone book. Finally she found Leo's number at the restaurant and punched in the numbers. *Oh, Leo,* she prayed, *be there tonight. Please, Leo.*

Andy, the maitre d', recognized Jane's voice. "Sure he's here, Miss Barnett. You hold on now and I'll get him on the line."

When he answered the phone Leo's voice lacked the usual exuberance he always had for customers.

"Leo, I can't find Max," Jane said frantically. "He was supposed to be here. An accident—" Her voice broke.

"Hey, Janie," Leo broke in. "Max is okay. Don't you worry."

"Where is he? What's wrong?"

Leo paused for a long moment. Then he spoke quietly and slowly. "He was here, honey. Stopped in to see me for a bit, as happy as a clam. You're sunshine to him, Janie. Sunshine and all sorts of other good things. But then that damn—excuse my French, Janie—that television over the bar came on and..." Leo stopped talking for a minute and cleared his throat. When he began again, his voice was low and clear. "Jane, he was here but then he left. He should be home now. Go to him, Janie."

Before Jane could ask any questions, Leo had hung up the phone.

Jane took off in her small car, not sure where she was going. She'd only been to Max's apartment once, on a sunny Saturday afternoon after Leo had taken all of them to an antique car race near Lake Geneva. They'd stopped at Max's on their way out of town to get some kites Max wanted to fly with Dewey. She concentrated hard on the memory of that fun-filled day and it helped block out some of the fear that was spreading through her like wildfire. She slowed down, searched for the next street sign in the murky darkness of the humid night, and then quickly drove on.

Thoughts raced through her mind but she couldn't make sense out of them. Not Leo's cryptic order, nor the fact that Max hadn't come or called.

But Max was safe; Leo had said so, and she knew from his voice it had to be true. Leo was distressed about something, but it wasn't the frantic distress he'd have if Max had been hurt.

The next street looked vaguely familiar, and Jane paused for a minute beneath the yellow glare of the streetlight, then turned right. Yes, this was it, this was Max's street. She knew because she had pointed out the elaborate facades on some of the brownstones, and Max had explained that it used to be one of Chicago's most elegant brothel districts. The very house his apartment was in used to be owned by Madam Julia, an elegant gray-haired lady. Her picture still hung in Max's study, and many pieces of her elegant, walnut furniture still graced his rooms.

Jane smiled, thinking of how she had tried not to look shocked, and how Max had then related the story of Julia's life, and done it as casually as if the madame had been an old family friend. He told of Julia's efforts to put three daughters through school and how one was now a circuit court judge.

Dear, wonderful Max, finding virtue in his resident ghost.

Her heart swelled. Please be okay, Max. Please, let everything be okay. She spotted the house then and quickly came to a stop at the curb. In seconds she was inside, taking the stairs two at once, until she arrived, breathless, at Max's door.

She knocked lightly. No one answered. When she knocked a second time the door moved slightly. She pushed it farther and stepped into the dark, carpeted hallway. The living room was just ahead. "Max?" she called softly. The name echoed loudly in the stillness of the apartment.

Jane walked quietly through the living room and down a wide hallway on the other side. She looked in the first door she came to. Like the other rooms in the house it was dark, but moonlight lit a single path across the hardwood floor. It passed over a small rug, an open bottle of Scotch, a half-filled glass. And then slanted across Max's shoes.

He sat on the end of his four-poster bed, his elbows on his knees, looking down at the pattern in the rug. He wore a rumpled suit, the jacket tossed carelessly on the bed, and the sleeves of his starched shirt were rolled up to his elbows.

"Max," she whispered.

He looked up at her, curiously for a moment, and then her presence seemed to register and he smiled crookedly. "Hi, Jane." His voice was profoundly sad.

Jane felt the breath leave her body. She moved over to his side and knelt down on the floor. He'd been drinking some but she didn't think he was drunk. "Max, what's happened?" An urge to wrap her arms around him overtook her, and she could feel her body begin to shake, but she stilled it, looked up at him and waited.

"My little Jane. You're beautiful in moonlight."

Jane half smiled, her eyes caressing his sad face.

Max turned his head and looked out the window. He took a drink of Scotch. "Jane, I'm sorry I missed our date tonight."

"It's okay, Max—"

"I was interrupted."

"I know. At Leo's."

He nodded. "It was the television. It did me in, Jane. I thought after all these years I had learned how to live with it. But there she was, on the screen. It was like yesterday."

"Who, Max?"

"Elizabeth. My wife Elizabeth." The last words were filled with pain.

Jane waited patiently, her heart wedged tightly in her chest. Finally Max began again.

"The local PBS station was doing a special on violent crime in the city over the past ten years. One of those violent crimes was Elizabeth's murder." His voice took on a low, calm tone as if he had repeated this story many, many times before. But the sadness tore at Jane's insides.

"On videotape, they showed her as they had found her that afternoon. She was taking the garbage out, this beautiful, young woman, carefree and happy. I was with the Chicago PD then, working on a case that was mob related. And I was afraid for Elizabeth, so I had arranged for her to go to her sister's house out in River Forest. She was supposed to stay there. But she didn't. She didn't trust me that it wasn't safe at home. So she went home to clean the house. *Clean the house.*" The words were repeated like a curse. "No one knew she'd gone back there." His voice cracked. He stopped for just a second, then took a deep breath, and continued.

"They got her when she came out the back door."

Jane wondered if there was enough air in the room for her to breathe. Finally she forced the words out. "But why, Max? Why Elizabeth?"

"We don't think they meant to get her. It was supposed to be me."

Jane leaned her head against his leg, but the movement did nothing to stop the tears that slid silently down her cheek.

"I've learned to live with it. For a while I didn't think I'd ever let myself love again, or be responsible again. Because I might fail, like I did Elizabeth. But then I met you. And I fell in love, Jane. And Dewey... Together you opened up those parts of me that had been closed to all feelings. And then when I saw her body on the television tonight, it—"

"You don't have to say any more, Max." Jane lifted herself to the bed and sat beside him. "I think I understand."

"I'm not really sure I do. But I had locked myself up so tightly that I had never allowed myself to grieve for her. Maybe I had to do that tonight."

Jane slipped into his arms. She could feel his hot tears slipping soundlessly into her hair. "Maybe so, Max. Maybe so."

For a long time they stayed that way, Jane wrapped in Max's arms, offering warmth and love to his grieving soul.

Finally she slipped from his embrace. "I'll make us some tea," she whispered into the darkness. "Why don't you rest for a while?" She pulled the bedclothes back. Max offered her a half smile, then leaned back against the headboard, exhausted.

When Jane returned a short while later his breathing had slowed, and some of the pain had eased from his face. His muscles were relaxed in sleep. She sat on the side of the bed and sipped the hot tea, and thought about Max's life. He'd lived with such great sorrow. And in spite of it, he had managed to love her. The thought kept coming back, again and again. Max had come to her with his own share of painful baggage, and she had never suspected it. He had managed to put it behind him.

She looked over at him one more time, and tears filled her eyes. "I love you, Max Harris," she whispered, and she leaned over and dropped a feathery kiss on his lips.

Max awoke slowly. He had a headache, and his mind was fuzzy. Slowly he pieced together the night before: Elizabeth's picture on the television, the terrible, gut-jerking pain that had passed through him as he'd stared at her lifeless body. He'd been racked with the guilt and sorrow that had plagued him for years. Sitting there in the bar, numb and grieving, he had thought of Jane. He knew in that moment of fresh grief that no matter what life dealt him, he loved her completely. He would risk the pain, the sorrow, anything, for that love.

Then he'd gone home and in the stillness of his apartment he'd been flooded with the enormity of his emotions, his terrible grief over Elizabeth's death, his love for Jane. Unable to sort them out, he'd sat in the darkness with his Scotch, his grief and his love.

And then she'd come out of the night. Jane—lovely, beautiful, compassionate Jane.

Max turned slightly in the wide bed. He tried to stretch his arm, only to press against something. Max turned onto his side and groped in the darkness, finding warm, smooth skin. His eyes shot open.

She was sleeping on her side, curled up beneath the sheet with one arm flopped carelessly over it. Her hair was a tangled silky mass against the white pillow, and her face was peaceful, her lips slightly parted. He stared hard at the curves outlined in the moonlight beneath the white sheet. She was beautiful. A sleeping angel.

Max slipped a finger beneath the sheet. Suddenly he was fully awake.

Jane was as naked as a newborn baby.

Nine

———

Max's throat went dry.

He thought he had imagined Jane in every way possible so that nothing would be a surprise. But the beauty of her body was beyond the limited range of his imagination. Jane was breathtaking. The faint light that filtered into the dark room fell across her smooth shoulders, and in the soft, gauzy light of predawn, she looked unreal, her body taking on the perfect carved contours of an alabaster statue.

With a gentleness Max didn't know he possessed, he brushed his fingertips along her shoulder. Images of sculptures faded quickly beneath his touch. No, this wasn't a statue. Jane's skin was warm and alive, beautiful, and as he watched her face, tiny movements flitted across her lips and eyelids in response to some dream.

Max wished he were there in the dream, loving her.

His gaze shifted again to her breasts. He wondered how long she'd been sleeping there beside him, it seemed the most astounding, unbelievable feat in the world that he could have slept, not knowing that Jane was lying next to him in his bed. He played with her hair, touching the silken strands with reverence. Her presence filled him more powerfully than a drug, and he settled back into the pile of cushions, content to watch her for a lifetime.

It might have been an hour later, Max wasn't sure, when Jane's eyelids quivered just slightly, and then slowly opened.

She looked up into the sea of his eyes, that clear midnight blue that had been with her in sleep. "Hi," she said shyly, pulling the sheet up across her breasts.

Max was still looking down at her. "Hi, yourself. Did I wake you?"

"Maybe, I don't know. I felt you here, I know that."

"Oh," Max said. And then he found himself at a complete loss for words. What did one say when one awoke and found an angel—a lovely naked angel— lying next to him. "Jane..." he began.

She smiled. It was a secret, sensual smile that dashed his resolve to stay calm. And then slowly and purposefully she lowered the sheet.

To Max it all seemed to happen in slow motion. He watched silently, his heart pounding while she let the sheet fall across her abdomen. She was exquisite. Her skin was firm and her breasts taut, the nipples already hardened by the chilly night air. She was more beautiful in life than he had imagined in any of his dreams.

He was afraid to touch her, afraid to disturb the moment.

"Max," Jane said huskily, "this isn't exactly how I planned it, but it'll be fine."

"Fine?"

"You and me. Here. The dinner you missed last night was the very first seduction dinner I've ever cooked. It's cold and stale, but I don't think I am."

Without a word he pulled her to him and buried his head in the hollow of her neck. Just the smell of her nearly drove him crazy. "No, Janie," he said, "I don't think you're cold and stale either."

"Good." Her hands were at the edge of his shirt, and she tugged lightly on it to pull it loose of his pants. "I got your shoes off after you fell asleep last night, but the rest was too much of a challenge."

"I'd say you're up to any challenge." Max shed his clothes. In seconds they were in a heap beside the bed. Then he paused for a moment.

Jane's hand went to his chest. She felt the threatening swell of tears, but she pushed them away. Her soft voice filled the heated air between them. "I knew you'd be magnificent, Max," she whispered. "I knew it...."

She moved her hand across his wide chest, idling to tug at the thick dark hair.

Max's breath caught in his throat. "Jane, you'd better watch it."

"I am," she said. And then her throaty laughter thrilled him as she scanned the length of him. "And I love what I see," she said.

Rivers of desire coursed through him. "Janie, I know . . . I know it's been a long time. I know it hasn't been easy for you. Are . . . are you sure about this?"

"Sure of what, Max?" Her eyes grew large, and for a moment she stopped her playful exploration. She looked into his eyes. "Sure that I love you? Yes. Absolutely sure. Sure that I want to make love tonight? I've never been more sure of anything in my life. I'm a little frightened, but I'm sure. And all the rest . . ." She bent down and dropped small kisses across his chest. When she pulled her head up again, her eyes were damp and shining. "All the rest, my love, is not for us to talk about tonight. Tonight is just for the two of us, just for loving."

Max pulled her to him then, too roughly at first, fueled by the enormity of his desire. And then he paused and held her with the care and gentleness he knew she needed. He fought the rushes of desire and sought only to please the woman who had turned his life from black and white to technicolor.

He held her as he would a precious gift, then bent his head and slowly began to kiss her breasts. At first he felt her stiffen, but in an instant the tension was gone, and in its place Max felt the quivering he knew to be the beginnings of desire.

He teased her nipples with his lips. "Oh, Max," she murmured against his ear. Her voice quivered. "You are so wonderful. So . . ."

Max didn't hear her ragged words; he heard only the rapid beating of her heart, and felt the pressure of her fingers digging into his hair. Slowly, as slowly as human valor allowed, he explored and brought pleasure to her flawless, lovely body, her breasts and the sweet-smelling valley between. With infinite slowness he kissed her breasts, closing his mouth over each nipple. Jane writhed with pleasure. Each time a new part of her was exposed to his caresses, tiny bolts of pleasure shot through her. His power was incredulous; with a touch, a kiss, a gentle thrust of his tongue, a streak of unimaginable pleasure filled her. She knew this loving was a gift, a very special gift. "Max," she said in a ragged voice, "this . . . this is a miracle, you know . . ."

"It takes two to make a miracle," Max said quietly. His words were followed by the hot trail of his tongue along her belly until Jane didn't think she could stand any more. But she did, and her heart swelled with each new sensation.

"My darling Jane," he said, his voice filled with emotion. "My love . . ."

Jane took his face in her hands and brought it up to hers. She ignored the tears that dampened her eyes. "Oh, Max," she said, her voice a soft cry, "I need you so very much."

He moved his powerful runner's thighs over her then and began to kiss the soft skin of her neck. He wanted to kiss her everywhere, to know every inch of her. And then he found her lips and slowly, profoundly, he showed her with a single kiss the depth of his love.

Jane could barely breathe. The trembling began in her toes and invaded every part of her body. She threw her arms around him and began a desperate exploration of his body. She sought out the narrowness of his waist, the firmness of his bottom.

"How did we get here to this heavenly place?" she asked. The voice that reached her ears was strange, unfamiliar and thick with the richness of desire.

"Getting here was easy, my love. Now we have to work on staying here. How about a lifetime or two?"

He licked her throat and then nipped lightly at her ear, and the heat in Jane's belly threatened to explode. She gulped in shallow breaths of air. "Oh, Max," she said, her voice trembling beneath the labored words, "let's not ever leave." She grasped his back, digging her fingers into his flesh with a hungry desperation. As he slid his body completely over hers, Jane felt herself soaring crazily. Stars spotted the darkness in front of her, and her body burned. She cried into the darkness. "Now, Max. Right now, oh, please—love me completely."

Max entered her slowly, focusing his eyes on her face. The feelings he was experiencing were reflected in her features, the joy, the passion, the raw need of their love.

Jane welcomed him with a passion born of this new love. Her emotions coursed through her, flowing through her fingers as she dug them into his back and swirling in the most hidden parts of her.

And then the force of their love split the night wide open. Lightning, thunder and the blare of a million trumpets filled Jane's ears and her limbs and her soul as she soared higher than a star. Then finally, bursting with Max's love, the earth and sky fell away. In slow motion they coasted together to the bed below.

They lay still and spent in each other's arms.

Jane couldn't speak. But when Max opened his eyes and looked down into her joyous face, there was no need for words.

He rolled over and wrapped her tightly in his arms, pressing her breasts to his chest, fitting her small hips tightly into the curve of his body. Jane was truly a part of him, he thought drowsily.

Hours later, when they awoke to birds and the sunlight that poured through the long east windows, they were still wrapped together.

"A Chinese egg roll," Jane murmured as she opened her eyes. She looked into Max's face just inches from her own.

"Hmmm?" He wove his fingers through her hair.

"That's what we are, a Chinese egg roll, all rolled together until you don't know what's what."

"A nice thought, being rolled together, I mean."

Jane nodded against his cheek. And then she lifted herself on one elbow to look down into his face. She touched his cheek with her fingers. "Max, I need to say something..."

Max heard the catch in her voice, and his heart slammed against his ribs. *No, Janie,* he prayed, *don't be sorry for this.*

"Max, I don't know what will come of us. But I love you. And I never thought, *never—*" her voice caught but she pushed on despite the growing lump in her throat, "—that I would be filled with such joy.

I...I thought that was for others, but not me. I thought something had died inside of me and that love like ours was never to be." The tears began to fall now, slowing winding down her cheeks.

Max caught a tear on the flat tip of his finger. Then he held her face gently between his palms and brought it down to his so he could kiss them all away.

She curled into the curve of his arm. "Thank you, Max," she whispered.

Max couldn't answer. There weren't words to explain the sensation of finding someone so special that she was now a part of him. There was too much joy, too much emotion to sort into words. So instead of talking, he held her gently in his arms until all the tears had fallen and they both fell back to sleep, their dreams peaceful.

Hours later, when Jane finally pulled herself from the haven of their bed, the sun was high in the sky and the radio broadcaster was talking about a heat wave.

"See what you've done, my love?" Max said. "The whole city is going to feel this now."

Jane padded softly across the bedroom floor. She wore nothing, not even a blush, and felt lovely in her nakedness. "I won't tell if you don't." She tossed her head, and her hair floated loosely about her shoulders. Jane couldn't remember ever having felt beautiful before. But today, with Max's eyes on her and his love inside of her, she knew she was exactly that.

Max leaned against the mountain of pillows, his arms folded across his chest. Just watching her brought him enormous pleasure. She moved like a dancer, graceful and smooth, as if a silent melody supported her. Whoever invented clothes had never seen Jane walk naked across his bedroom floor, he thought. He wondered if she would ever look other than the way she did right now, all peaches and cream, curves and delicate rises.

"I feel your smile, my sweet gumshoe," she said. She stopped walking and turned around. "A breakfast for your thoughts."

"My thoughts are of a lovely, passionate accountant."

Jane's eyebrows raised. "Oh? Not possible. Contradiction in terms."

Max edged off the bed and walked toward her. "So I used to think."

"And now?" Jane's heartbeat quickened.

"Now I think that I know a secret about accountants and all that figuring they do. And I'll never tell a soul." He opened his arms and she moved into them readily.

She burrowed her head into his chest and began to nibble lightly at his skin. "So, about breakfast. Eggs, bacon, pancakes? I'm starved." She lifted her head and caught the tip of his ear in her teeth.

Max stiffened and swallowed a groan. "I think I've created a monster," he said.

"Nope. I've always liked big breakfasts." She slipped her hands around his waist, and when he lifted her off the ground, Jane decided there were some things in life more important than hardy breakfasts.

Ten

"You know, Sara, it's a little like releasing a bag of feathers on the top of a windy hill."

Sara laughed and reached for another blueberry muffin. They were sitting in a sidewalk café on a warm July day watching Chicago life stream by.

"I mean, they're leaving, Sara. All those horrible demons. One by one."

"It's about time, hon. You've lived with them far too long."

"A lifetime." Jane took a bite of her chicken salad. Then she stopped and laughed. "Even chicken tastes different."

"I remember when I first fell in love with George," Sara said. "I had this thing for jelly beans. All those fruit flavors. I wanted to try each one because the tastes were so great and I couldn't get enough of them. I gained ten pounds." She looked at her friend and smiled. "It's definitely affected you, but not in the fat department."

Jane smiled. No, she hadn't gained weight, although her body had changed in other ways. She was aware of parts of herself she'd given little thought to in the past years, and sometimes she wondered if people sensed it in business meetings or the grocery store. "I feel like Sleeping Beauty. I've been asleep for so long . . ."

Sara had been listening carefully, her mind filled with bothersome thoughts. Now she stopped eating and looked at her friend gravely as she wrapped her fingers around the cool glass of iced tea. "You know, Janie, Max is truly a terrific man."

Jane was puzzled. Sara's comment didn't fit smoothly into their conversation. It was said seriously, with an ominous tone. "Sara, if I know anything, I know that. Max is the best thing that ever happened to me."

"That's an understatement. He's the once-in-a-lifetime kind of guy. Like George. Max has taught you how to live again, Jane. You're different now; I'm not even sure you know *how* different, but George and I see it, and Dewey senses it, too."

Jane sipped her lemonade slowly. Sara was right. Of course she was different. She was learning to love, to trust all over again. Max was opening up a world she had nearly forgotten existed.

"I don't mean that you weren't quite wonderful before, Jane," Sara went on. "You were. I certainly wouldn't have picked anyone but the best to be my closest friend. But you were cheating yourself all those years. And then Max came along and..." Sara paused, as if choosing her words carefully. "Max has helped you pull yourself out of hell, Janie. George and I tried to, but we could only go so far. But Max has done it. You know that, don't you?"

Jane looked at Sara long and hard, trying to read her friend's thoughts. She wasn't saying what she wanted to say, and that wasn't like Sara at all. "Sara, you're talking in circles. What are you getting at?"

Sara played with the food on her plate with her fork. Finally she looked up at Jane. "I guess what I'm saying is, I think you need to be careful here. Max needs—expects, deserves, whatever you want to call it—all of you. All your trust and love. He's...he's that kind of person. And he should get that—all or nothing."

Jane sat back in the chair. Damn Sara. Damn her for reading thoughts that weren't public domain. Every day with Max, every night, every minute made Jane think the same thing. The more she loved Max, the more she knew he deserved a total love, no strings, no conditions, no holdbacks. And she really thought, most of the time anyway, that she could handle it. There weren't many doubts left, only a few. And she was sure she could manage those.

"Jane, if I'm out of line," Sara said. Then she stopped and shook her head. "No, I'm *not* out of line so I won't apologize. I'm your best friend, and I care a lot for Max. So that gives me some rights. I'm just afraid, Janie..." She reached out suddenly and took her friend's hand. "I'm afraid sometimes that you haven't quite learned to trust him totally. And he deserves it, Janie. You have to give it to him.''

That night when Dewey had been picked up by the Jennings for his weekly Tuesday night outing, Jane drove over to Max's. He'd insisted she come for dinner and he would serve his specialty—Chinese takeout.

Jane sat at the round oak table while Max opened up a half-dozen square white boxes. The fragrance of velvet chicken and Moo Shoo pork floated about the kitchen. Jane watched Max and sought to put her feelings in place. Sara's words echoed uncomfortably in her head. There was no question of love; she loved Max so much she felt sure it was emblazoned across her forehead in red paint. And surely people had noticed the swelling in her heart and the silly smile she wore at odd times.

But Sara was right. Max deserved the kind of love that was supported by complete trust. Was that the kind of love she was feeling?

She watched him fill two plates full of the Chinese food. Every now and then he tossed a sliver to Potter.

At times, fearful images still haunted the fringe of her conscious thoughts, but what did they matter in the middle of all of this? It was Craig's awful legacy, and it faded to almost nothing next to the brilliance of her love for Max.

Max handed her the plate, and for a while the troubling thoughts were dimmed by the pungent flavors.

"Well, Janie," Max asked a while later, "What'll it be?" Potter was busy cleaning the last remnants of food from their plates, and Jane was wiping the table. Max stood in front of the freezer, surveying possible desserts.

"Surprise me," she said, and turned her back to rinse out the sink.

"Okay." Max let the refrigerator door swing closed and had circled the table before she realized what was happening. And then, while Potter sat in the corner and watched approvingly, Max lifted her off the floor and walked out the door.

"Max!" she said, her voice breaking with laughter. "You're crazy. What are you doing?"

Max called hello to several elderly neighbors strolling down the street. They all smiled as he walked by, carrying the attractive young woman in his arms. Max no longer surprised them; they were amused by the tall, friendly man who often helped them repair steps and fix ornery locks.

"Max, answer me," Jane said as his footsteps quickened and he gripped her tighter against his chest.

"I'm going to surprise you. Wasn't that what you said?" His voice was deep and suggestive.

"I'm too heavy, Max—"

"Nah. A mere wisp," he said. "Okay, Janie, here we are."

Jane pulled her head away from his shoulder and looked around. They were at the end of the next block, and across the street was the train station.

Max lowered her to the ground, and soon she stood on her own. "Well, you're right, Max. Here we are." She looked up at him. "But *where* are we, exactly?"

"The train. It stops here."

Jane stood on tiptoe and looked closely at his face. "Are you all right? It's been hot. Maybe this is heat stroke."

Her words were drowned out by the arrival of the southbound train, and before Jane could stop him, Max had taken her hand and pulled her across the street.

By the time she found herself in the sleek silver car, Jane had decided not only that Max was crazy, but that she must have something slightly loose herself. She was loving the absurdity, the spontaneousness of Max's actions.

"This is, as Dewey would say, bizarre," Jane said, laughing. She slid over to the window and made room for Max to fold his long body next to her. "But I have to admit, life with you, Max Harris, is never dull."

Max looked around. The car was nearly empty. He lifted her hair from her neck and whispered into her ear. "I've been wanting to get you alone on the southbound since I first laid eyes on you."

Jane giggled as his breath sent shivers racing up and down her spine. He wrapped his arm around her and held her close while the train picked up speed.

"Alone at last." He sighed.

Jane looked across the aisle at two young teenage boys who hadn't taken their eyes off of them for a single moment.

"Well, not quite," she whispered.

Max looked over at the kids. "Hi, fellas."

No answer.

"Going far?"

The taller youth shrugged and lit up a cigarette while the other one pulled a beer from beneath his jacket and took a quick gulp.

Max pulled a pencil from his pocket. "Maybe you wouldn't mind helping us out with this survey. We're with the Northwestern security patrol, doing a little investigation into who uses the trains after eight at night. We're supposed to question every passenger. All we need are your names, addresses and answers to a couple of questions...."

The two youths were already out of their seats. "Sorry, man, we gotta get off here...."

And when the train pulled into its next stop, Max and Jane found themselves the sole passengers in the brightly lit car.

"You're downright devious." Jane nudged him in the side. "Those poor kids. You scared the wits out of them."

"Nah, kids don't scare that easily. They took one look at you and knew I wanted to be alone to do this..." Max leaned over, and as the train pulled slowly away from the station, he kissed her. It was a slow, passionate kiss, filled with sweet familiarity.

Jane wove her fingers through his hair and welcomed the taste of him. Passion awoke instantly. That's what it was like now between them, a look, a word, a touch—and the skies lit up like the fourth of July. Finally Jane pulled away. "Max Harris, what was my life like before I met you?" She settled back in his arms while the northern suburbs swept by outside the window.

Max pondered her question with exaggerated attention. "Well," he said finally, his brow furrowing, "you probably didn't take trains to get hot-fudge sundaes."

"Is that what we're doing?"

"Among other things. There's an old drugstore in Highland Park that makes its own fudge sauce. They have a sundae called Luscious Lovers' Delight." He rubbed the back of her neck lightly.

"Shouldn't it be lovers' luscious delight."

"Depends. I'd say you're pretty luscious."

"Oh...you're...just saying...that..." While she tried to talk, Max inched his fingers beneath her sweater, and the words came out in starts and stops.

"Nope." Max kissed her nose, the top of her head and then the tender skin of her neck. "Definitely luscious."

"Oh, Max... I'm going to be a melted mess in a minute...." She took several deep breaths of air. "I...I don't know how you do this to me..."

"Like this..." Max touched the tip of her breasts with his fingers and made slow, teasing circles.

Jane wrapped her arms around his neck and pulled him close. He could arouse her, he could comfort her, he could make her laugh. But mostly he could make her love again. "Max Harris, I love you," she whispered into the hollow of his neck. "I love you very much."

Max sat back and cupped her chin in his palm, looking down into her sea green eyes. ''Maybe we should talk about that, Jane.''

She nodded.

''We can't just let all that love float around forever. We need to give it a shape.''

''Yes, we do.'' Her words were barely audible.

Max took a deep breath. He wanted to marry her. There was no question in his mind. He wanted to include her and Dewey into his life for the rest of time. And he wanted Jane to want it as deeply and unconditionally as he did. He knew that was the only way it would work.

The train began to slow down, and the sign for Highland Park appeared beside the window.

''Jane,'' Max said slowly, ''you need to give that some thought, but not tonight. Tonight's for hot fudge and cherries and whipped cream. But soon, Janie, soon.''

Jane stood and walked slowly to the double doors. She stood there beside Max while the world outside whizzed by unnoticed. Give shape to that love, he had said. Give commitment to it, was what he meant. She wanted to do that very badly, but had to be sure she could. He said she could deal with it later—maybe she would sort it out in the quiet of the night.

She hooked her arm in his and stepped from the train in search of a more immediate reality, like Chicago's finest hot-fudge sundae.

''Nope, can't go out to eat with you, Mom.''

"Dewey, since when have you been making your own plans? You're only six, you know."

Dewey grinned at his mother feigned irritation. His glasses slipped down until they rested on a nest of freckles at the tip of his nose. "I'm only doing it for Uncle Leo. He hasn't been to the museum in *ages*." Dewey drew out the last word to be sure Jane understood the incredible importance of it all. If Dewey missed a month at the Museum of Science and Industry, he made Jane feel that, at the least, she ought to wear black.

"Okay. I understand, kiddo. I wouldn't want to deprive Uncle Leo of anything that important."

"And besides," Dewey said with a noticeable twinkle in his eye, "you and Max don't need us to have fun."

Jane looked at him sideways.

Dewey stopped fiddling with his microscope and looked at her gravely. He frowned a little, and Jane realized with a start that it was Max's expression she was seeing on her son's face. It was that earnest look Max got when he wasn't kidding around any longer.

"I like Max, Mom," Dewey said now. His eyes filled the circles of his glasses. "A whole lot."

Jane felt a lump in her throat. In the beginning she had thought a lot about Dewey's reaction to Max. She had been cautious about the amount of time they spent together, not wanting Dewey to get attached prematurely. And then it had all fallen apart when she found herself in love with this man who had come to her out of a pile of messed-up receipts. The caution she had carefully nursed disappeared in the flash of

Max's lopsided grin. Dewey said he liked Max a lot. But Dewey didn't need to say a word. She knew he was crazy about Max. And Max felt the very same way about him.

"Well, Dewey," she said, the strange lump still there, "I know that. I know you like him. And I do, too." Now tears threatened, and Jane had no earthly idea why. She began to brush her hair vigorously.

"And he likes us," Dewey said confidently.

Jane nodded, not wanting to speak, and not knowing what to say even if she could speak.

Yes, Max was absolutely right, it was time to make a commitment, and this waiting for the Lord Himself to come down and tell her it was the absolute, certain, right thing to do, and that she'd never endanger Dewey and herself again, was ridiculous. She needed to exorcise that last bastion of fear and move ahead with her life. It was time.

She and Max had dinner at a new dockside restaurant near the marina, and Jane felt lighthearted and in love. The night was perfect: a full moon, a clear, cool, velvet sky and Max.

"'A loaf of bread, a jug of wine, and thou beside me in the wilderness'," said Max. "Pretty nice."

Jane narrowed a look at him, unnerved by his ability to read her mind. "You do that so easily it frightens me sometimes. What if I didn't want you to know what I was thinking?"

"Sometimes you do," Max said simply. "I ignore those thoughts. It's called selective telepathy."

"Well, see that it stays that way, bub."

Max laughed. Jane's acting tough always made him smile. No matter how hard she tried, she always failed miserably. She couldn't shake that Grace Kelly image.

"Max," Jane said suddenly, "has it ever occurred to you that we don't know each other's middle names?"

"Not recently." Max sat back in the chair, amused.

"Or that I don't know your favorite color?"

"The color of your eyes."

"Or song."

"Some Enchanted Evening."

"Or movie star," Jane persisted.

"Who needs movie stars? I've got Janie."

"Or whether you were an athlete or a brain or a troublemaker when you were in tenth grade."

"That's a tough one. I do remember a while there when I went to school on Saturdays for some reason..."

"Max, I'm halfway serious. Our lives are becoming more and more entwined, and there are things—"

"—that don't matter a whole lot, Jane. People decide to spend the rest of their lives together so they can discover things like that. If we knew everything about each other now, it'd spoil the fun."

Jane slowly sipped her coffee. The rest of their lives. People did decide that. She was living so fully in the present she didn't think about forever.

"You're right, Max," she finally agreed. "I think it's the accountant in me wanting everything to fit neatly into its place."

"And unfortunately, Janie, life isn't always like that. You can't know the score of tomorrow's Cubs game today. We know the important things about each other."

Jane folded her napkin and set it beside her plate. She knew she loved him. That was certainly important. Yes, Max was right.

"I'm sorry, Max," she said slowly. "Sometimes I get a little crazy."

"Yeah." He reached out and took her hand. "But I like it. Crazy looks good on you. So will this."

He slipped his free hand into his pocket and pulled out a small box. Jane looked at it, then up at Max. "Max, how nice. But why? It's not my birthday—"

"I know. You're a Libra—probably around the twenty-eighth of September or so."'

He laughed when her mouth fell open, and he decided not to tell her Dewey had revealed certain personal facts to him one day when they had gone to the zoo.

"Max, how—"

"Parlor trick," he said. "But open the box. It's not a special occasion present."

"But—"

Max tapped her mouth closed. "Just take it, Jane. And say 'thank you, Max.'"

Jane's mouth relaxed in a smile. It was these little gestures that did her in, these small signs of affection. She had lived without them for so long. And now Max had shown her this unfamiliar side of love. She looked up at him. "Okay. Thank you, Max." She lifted his fingers to her lips and kissed them, then picked up the box and lifted off the top.

"Max!"

Max watched her face and marveled at her pleasure. She was like a child at times like this, a beautiful, innocent child.

Carefully, as if she thought it would disappear with too much handling, Jane lifted the gift from the box. On a tiny gold chain a jeweler had carefully placed each of the crinoids Max and Jane had found at the lake. They were attached directly to links so that each small shell hung alone on the necklace.

Jane touched them gingerly with the tip of her finger. "I remember this one especially," she said softly, singling out a shell. "It's the one you challenged the wave for—"

"And won, I might add," Max said.

"Of course," Jane said, her eyes still on the necklace, her heart full. "Max, this is beautiful." When she lifted her eyes to him, they spoke to Max more eloquently than her words.

He nodded. "I thought you might like it."

Jane lifted it to her neck and closed the tiny gold clasp in the back. The necklace hung down on top of her blue silk blouse. "It's perfect." She leaned over the small table and kissed him, ignoring completely the surprised, curious smiles of the other diners.

"The fossils are nearly as old as our love," Max said when they pulled apart.

"That old, huh?"

"Yep. I think what we have has been floating around in the universe, just waiting for the two of us to catch it."

"Well, if that's true," Jane said, "I'm sorry it took so long."

"All that matters is that it's here."

"Yes," Jane whispered.

"And that it stays," Max said, and then he picked up the check and motioned for the waiter.

Jane stood on the sidewalk outside the restaurant a short while later and waited while Max went to get the car. The parking lot was full of puddles so Max had insisted she stay there and wait for him. That way she wouldn't get wet feet. He had laughed lightly at the double meaning, and Jane had been left fingering her necklace, content with his chivalry.

She looked up at the flickering sky and concentrated on the stars and the planets. They were the same ones they'd looked at from the grassy rise at the farm that day so many eons ago, and the thought gave her a strange sense of well-being. Had it been that day at the farm that she had fallen in love with Max? She had no idea. It could have been any moment since the day Max first left a message on her answering machine.

She fingered her necklace and pondered the thought. The tiny crinoids were cool and smooth at her throat. Did a person fall in love in a day or an instant? Or was it a cumulative thing, like a rolling stone? Love. Such a strange emotion and with about as many facets as those stars. Love had filled her life, and she wondered if she had ever felt this way before.

For the first time in many weeks Jane thought of Craig Barnett. His handsome smiling face came to her so suddenly that tiny goose bumps stood up on her arms and she rubbed them vigorously to dispel the chill. Craig... She squeezed her eyes shut and tried to block his image from her mind, but it stuck there like the residue from sticky tape. Had she ever loved Craig? Her mind wanted to say no, but the truth was that she had. She had loved him and had trusted him.

Jane squeezed her eyes tighter, but the horrible images refused to disappear. The harder she tried, the more vivid they were: Craig raging because his vegetables were cold. Craig locking her out of the house because Dewey had been cranky with teething and she had forgotten to buy any beer that day. He had headed for Dewey's crib, his mind fogged by drink, his irrational laughter drifting out the window where she stood paralyzed by fear. He had picked Dewey up and held him in front of the window. "You want him so much, Janie?" he had said. "Right now? Wanna catch?"

At that moment Jane knew there had to be a God, because Craig turned then and staggered back to the crib where he placed the baby on the soft blue blanket. Dewey had slept through the incident.

That was the night Jane left.

Jane was so buried in the painful memories she didn't see the man come out of the shadows. She didn't hear his soft footsteps on the sidewalk. It was the odor that first pulled her out of the past. The odor of unwashed skin and booze. Jane froze. Before she could move, the man had pressed himself against her back, one hand around the strap of her purse, the other at her shoulder. She felt cold, sharp steel on the back of her neck. "Your purse, lady, gimmee it."

Jane didn't have time to react. At that moment Max drove up in front of the restaurant. He spotted her immediately—spotted the shadowy figure at her back. With the engine left running he leaped from the car and raced toward Jane.

Desperate, the derelict pressed the knife harder against Jane's neck. "Gettaway," he snarled as Max approached, but his sluggish words were lost on Max.

Max's nerves were raw with fear for Jane's safety. No one would hurt her, ever. In a movement so swift the thief barely saw it, Max pushed him clear of Jane. The man stumbled and fell toward the cement, but before his limbs hit ground, Max lifted him again. And then while Jane watched, her back pressed tight against the brick building, Max raised his fist and pummeled the man's chest, throwing him to the ground. Max stood over the dazed man, his eyes filled with rage as he lifted his hand again.

Jane watched in horror. A cry rose from her throat but no sound came from her. She could see him coming at her, Craig, his blond hair still in place, a smile on his face. He was coming toward her with his large hands curled into fists. She leaned back against the countertop of their tiny kitchen, but she couldn't stop him. Nothing could stop him.

And as Max's knuckles met the loose jaw of the disheveled vagrant, she felt the full force of the blow. For a minute she stood there, and then her mind went blank. Jane fainted onto the cold, unforgiving pavement.

* * *

She had awakened in Max's car, but it wasn't until she saw her house, the porch light, the familiar green door, that Jane allowed her mind to function. She was home. She was safe.

Max led her inside and over to the striped couch in the living room. When he covered her with the blanket, she nodded, then closed her eyes and tried to stop shivering. A chill had invaded her bones, had gripped her heart. Nothing felt the same.

Max pulled up an old rocking chair and sat at her side, smoothing out the blanket with his large hands. "I'm so sorry, Jane," he whispered. "So sorry—"

"No, Max," she said. She tried to smile, but her lips wouldn't work. "You didn't—"

"I should never have left you. If anything had happened..." And then his face seemed to fall.

"Nothing happened. I'm fine, Max," she whispered. But she didn't feel fine and the shaking wouldn't stop. She felt ravaged by fear, but even more by the memories that had ripped her world apart. Her demons weren't dead, not by a long shot.

"If I had been any later..." Max's words were lost in the sadness.

"Max, don't." Jane couldn't talk anymore. The derelict had shaken her severely, but he was gone. The terrible anguish that was strangling her had resulted from Max's raised fist, from the anger that had filled every inch of him, from the violence in this gentle man that she loved.

When she finally fell off to sleep Max was still there. He wouldn't leave her alone. Much later he moved her to her bed, and when she awoke during the night, she saw him sleeping in the wicker chair beside the bed, his long legs stretched out on the floor in front of him. For hours she watched him and loved him and grieved for what she knew now couldn't be. Craig truly had ruined her. He had implanted in her a fear so grave that she couldn't give Max what he deserved. How could she trust him completely now?

Tears slid noiselessly down her cheeks and onto the white pillow. Her love, her wonderful, sweet love.

In the morning she insisted she was fine and that Max should leave. Leo would be bringing Dewey home soon. She had a pile of work to do.

Her sad smile sent him away feeling chilled.

That night Max came by with a pizza and a container full of white chocolate mousse yogurt.

"Jane," he said, "when Dewey goes to bed, we need to talk."

"Yes," she said quietly.

Once Dewey was asleep, they sat in separate chairs in front of the fireplace on a ninety-two degree summer evening, and Jane was chilled to the core. She wrapped her arms around herself and fought the tears behind her eyelids.

"Jane," Max said, leaning toward her, his elbows braced by his knees, "you're hurting—"

"I'm not hurt, Max," she said softly. "I'm all right."

"No, you're not. But this time I don't think I can help."

Jane shook her head no.

"No, I can't help?"

"Max—"

"Janie," he said, not wanting to make her explain. "Jane, I hit that man because I love you. I didn't think about what I did, I just did it. It was the fastest way to stop him."

Jane nodded. Her eyes stung painfully. She knew every single word he said was true, but it didn't change anything. It didn't kill the ugly fear that had gripped her when she saw his hand curl into a fist. It didn't erase the memories of another man, a man she had once loved, threatening Dewey's life with his anger.

"I can't take it back," Max went on slowly, "and I can't even promise it won't happen again, because it might. If you or Dewey were threatened, and the fastest, surest way to protect you was to hurt someone else, I would to it, Jane." He stopped talking then, and slumped in the chair, spent. For the first time in the past forty hours, Max admitted to himself that they might not have a future.

Jane saw how exhausted he was. His whole body looked limp, that wonderful, strong body that had brought her such incredible joy.

"Max, it's not you, it's me. I'm handicapped as surely as if I had lost a vital part of my body. I can't get rid of the fear Craig pounded into me. I thought I could, but I can't." Her voice dropped to a whisper. "I love you more than I ever dreamed possible, but I can't believe the violence won't happen again. There's something in me, Max, something horrible that cuts off part of my heart...."

Max fought the overwhelming urge to take her in his arms, but he wouldn't do it this time. This time Jane held all the cards.

"It doesn't make sense," Jane said softly.

"Yes, it makes sense. Part of it anyway." He searched her face, hoping against reason that he would find the right words there. "Your fear makes sense. That's real. What doesn't make sense is your accepting it. You're letting Craig win, Jane."

"It's not a contest, Max."

"No, but you're making it into one. You're making it a contest between me and Craig. And I don't have a chance because the guy I'm fighting is in your head. He's not real anymore, Jane. Let him go, damn it."

The anguish on her face stopped him. He stared at his shoes, at the lines in the hardwood floor. Jane had become his life, that remarkable thing the poets talked about, and now she was being torn from him. And for the second time in his life, Max felt totally helpless.

He rose slowly from the chair, feeling years older. "I've hurt you with my words, Janie. I didn't mean to." His voice was calm, the agony lying just below the surface.

Jane couldn't look up.

"I'm going to go, Jane. I love you, and I pray to God you'll be able to see things differently."

Her voice came out in sobs. "I can't Max. I simply can't."

Max walked toward the door, but he couldn't feel anything. Not the floor, nor the handle, nor the hot summer night. Holding the door open, he turned to look at her.

Jane hadn't moved. She sat beside the fireplace, her face drained of color, her eyes swollen with tears.

"Jane, I'll be there for you."

"Goodbye, Max," she whispered.

Eleven

Dewey stayed at the Jennings' for three days.

"I'm sorry, Jane, but he's hurt and angry." Sara stood at the door to Jane's bedroom, her hands curled into fists at her hips. "And if you didn't look so godawful miserable yourself, I'd have to join his camp. I don't understand, Janie."

The tears began again, falling down her cheeks in rivers. There were times during the past week that Jane had marveled at the enormous amount of moisture that could be stored in the human body. But those were isolated moments of sanity. For most of the week she had walked through the days carefully, filling out clients' financial statements, answering business calls, cleaning her house, and all the while grieving for a loss so great she didn't think she could get through the hour.

Dewey had been devastated. "But even though Max and I aren't going to be going out," Jane said as calmly and gently as her fractured sensibilities would allow, "you and Max will always be friends. And next week Uncle Leo is planning a whole day of things for you to do together."

But none of it made sense to the small boy, and he made excuses to be at the Jennings, away from Jane and the mess she had made of his life.

"Jane," Sara was saying beside her, "try to talk to me. Just try to make me understand, hon. Maybe I can help." Sara slipped down on the bed beside her.

"It's what you said, Sara. It's giving Max what he deserves—my trust and love. One was easy, but the other..." Her voice broke, and Sara slipped an arm around her shaking shoulders. "I really loved Craig once, Sara—you know that's true. I can't remember it with my heart anymore—there's too much pain there now. But I know I did—"

"Yes," Sara said quietly. "You did love Craig."

"I can't imagine I loved him like I do Max, but there was something there. And then look what he did, Sara..." Tears slid down her face.

"It's okay, hon. Here..." Sara plucked a tissue from the box and shoved it into Jane's hand.

Jane blew her nose. "I thought what I did was right. But then why do I feel this way, Sara? Why do I feel like my guts have been stomped on and my heart cut in half? Without him, Sara, it just doesn't work..."

"Now that's something to think about, isn't it? You know, Jane, you've always been smarter than I—but for all those smarts, sometimes you don't see the forest for the trees."

"Oh, I see him, Sara. I see him when I'm awake, asleep, when I'm crying or just being miserable—"

"What you don't see is something that is as plain as the nose on your face. You're no longer the same person who loved Craig Barnett, Jane. You were just a kid when you met him. And even if you weren't, Craig was *sick*, and he hid that sickness from you.

"Life is full of risks, Janie. You can avoid them and walk that narrow, careful path, or you can jump onto one or two and move out into a world that just might bring you a whole hell of a lot of happiness. It's a choice, Janie. You know, I knew about Craig when I fell in love with George. I knew about the horrible things he did to you. But my turning away from George because of the Craigs of this world would have made about as much sense as your turning from Max." She was holding Jane by the shoulders now, trying desperately to reach beyond the grief to some tiny light of reason.

Jane lifted her head slowly. "It's simple, isn't it, Sara? But there's one difference..." Her eyes were large and round and sad in her narrow face.

"What's that, sweetie?"

"Craig didn't injure you, Sara. You weren't left damaged goods."

Dewey came home on Friday, and Jane tried with every ounce of strength she had in her to smile and assure him their life would be happy and full.

She made fried chicken, stocked up on favorite videos and told him he could have soda for dinner instead of milk.

When she called him in to eat, Dewey walked through the door slowly and then stood in the middle of the kitchen staring at his tennis shoes. "I'm sorry," Dewey said.

"For what, honey?"

"I lost my glasses."

Jane stood at the sink, her heart reaching out to him. "Glasses?" she said. And then she walked over to him, kneeled down and took him in her arms. "That's okay. We can get more."

Dewey pulled away. "Get mad, Mom! You're supposed to get mad when I lose my glasses!" And he turned from her and bolted from the room.

Jane stood in the silent kitchen and stared at the pan of chicken. When the tears came she let them run down her shirt and onto the well-swept floor. At least Dewey had his anger to help him through this.

Hours later Jane sat on the ground in her small garden and breathed in the smell of damp earth. Beams of moonlight fell across her knees and shoulders. She looked up at the half sphere of the moon and sought the smiling face of the man up there who had given her peculiar comfort when she was a child. He was still smiling, and that fact made Jane smile, too.

Inside Dewey was sleeping soundly. Through the open window she could hear the small noises he made in sleep. She and Dewey had stayed up late watching an old movie Jane had rented. It was a kids' movie about a little girl unintentionally kidnapped by two bumbling, likable crooks. And in the subplot the little girl's mother left the self-serving politician father and began a new life with the kind, handsome policeman.

"Did you like it?" she had asked Dewey as they cleaned up the popcorn dishes before bed.

"Yeah," he said. "I liked the people. They made mistakes—like the mom—and then she went back and changed things so they worked better. And they risked stuff, like the crooks when they gave the little girl back even though they might get in trouble."

And then he'd hugged her, a brief tight hug, and had run off to bed.

Risks and correcting mistakes were on Dewey's mind. Jane dug her fingers into the earth and thought of that, of risks and mistakes and putting it all back together. Humpty Dumpty, she thought. Was it too late to put the pieces back together? Would it take all the king's men, or could she do it by herself?

The long sad week had taught her many things, but the most important lesson was that she wasn't the same without Max. And it wasn't just the overwhelming sadness; no, it went way beyond that. Max made her feel alive, he brought with him good times, laughter and spontaneity. He filled the days with a richness that she had lived without for so long she hadn't missed it. Until Max. And now she missed it so dreadfully her heart ached and her body was as hollow as a wind tunnel.

She hugged her knees to her chest and looked beyond the thick mass of impatiens and begonias that Max had helped her plant. Growth, she thought. He had helped her grow. With Max's love inside her, she had grown beyond Craig Barnett and the agony of that other life. With Max's love . . .

The tears began to fall again, down her cheeks and knees and onto the cool earth. But along with the tears her heart was swelling, filling again with hope. With Max's love she could do most anything—if she was willing to try.

And as the clouds cleared and the golden light of the moon fell upon her, the fuzziness left her head and her heart. Sara was right. She hadn't seen the forest for the trees. She hadn't considered what Max's love had done for her, how it had given her a new life, had changed her, had healed her. And she had thrown it all away! But maybe it wasn't too late. Maybe she still had a chance. She had hurt Max terribly, but she'd make it all up to him. Yes, she promised, she would.

She got up from the ground and looked back up at the smiling face of the moon. "Yes, big fella," she said out loud, her head pulled back and her face turned up to the light. "I love him. I love him!"

The tears began again when she reached the phone, but it didn't matter anymore. Nothing mattered but reaching Max, loving Max, and asking him to forgive her. She dialed three times to make sure the number was right, then hung up. He wasn't there. It was three o'clock in the morning and Max wasn't there. And he hadn't even turned on his answering machine. Leo's she thought. He might be out at Leo's, but it was too late to call there, so she hugged her love to herself and fell into a restless sleep.

Dewey had left in the morning to spend the day at the farm. Sara had been insistent that Jane go along, but when she'd seen the new glimmer in Jane's eyes, she had changed her mind. "Stay here," Sara had said. "And be constructive." She'd hugged Jane tightly, grabbed Dewey's hand and left.

By midafternoon Jane couldn't handle the pacing any longer so she got in her car and drove to Max's apartment. Mrs. Atchity, the tiny gray-haired lady who managed the building, told Jane her knocking wouldn't be heard in South Bend, and since that's where Max was, she might as well stop making all that racket.

Jane dropped her hand.

"He'll be back presently," Mrs. Atchity went on, "so you go ahead and leave a little note, dearie, and stick it right there under the brass knocker. And make it cheery." She pursed her lips together then and looked at Jane sternly. "He's been unhappy, young lady, and that's not a good way to be. So you go on now and write that note."

"Yes, ma'am," Jane said meekly.

"Dear Max," she wrote, and then stopped. Her mind raced. *Dear Max, dear, dear Max. I love you Max. I love you more than you can imagine. And I'll be good for you, Max, I promise you that.* A new batch of tears began to well up behind her lids, and Jane turned away from the door and walked on down the steps. No, a piece of paper was not the way to do it. She needed to see him, to show him in her eyes and her face how much she loved him. Jane wadded the paper up into a tiny ball and stuffed it in her pocket.

She fixed a peanut butter and jelly sandwich for her dinner and then sat at the window with the uneaten sandwich beside her. *Presently.* Mrs. Atchity had said he'd be back presently. What did that mean? Today? Tomorrow? Never? Might Max never come back to her?

Her heart twisted and turned beneath the thought. The pain was so strong Jane thought she was going to be sick. No! He had to come back to her. She had to convince him they could work out all their problems together, but only together, because without Max she was half of a person.

The sky began to darken outside the window, and Jane lowered her head on the ledge. Presently. Max would come to her presently. She shut her eyes and blocked out the sounds of the world and filled her sleepy head with the only thoughts that mattered now.

It wasn't the uncomfortable press of her chest against the window sill that woke her two hours later. It was a sound so piercing that her heart clamored against her rib cage as she shot upright in the chair. And then her chest constricted and her whole body shook with painful coughs.

Jane's eyes shot open, then stung fiercely as they were assaulted by huge curls of smoke billowing into the room.

She stifled a cry and rushed for the door.

The clean white house on Greendale Lane was on fire.

Twelve

Jane stood on the lawn and stared at the confusion in front of her. Firemen were everywhere, their uniformed bodies efficiently dismantling her house and dousing the flames that had leaped to life from a bad electrical connection in the kitchen.

Tears streamed down her face. It's not so bad, a fireman had comforted her. She was one of the lucky ones.

Lucky, she thought, shoving her hands into the pockets of her jeans. Lucky? She had driven away the one man in the world who filled her with joy. And now her house was filled with black, billowy smoke. But Dewey was safe. She was safe. And Max—somewhere in South Bend or God-knows-where—Max was safe. Even if he never spoke to her again, he was safe, and suddenly the importance of that filled her with joy. She wiped away the dampness with the back of her hand and felt a new batch of tears begin their well-rehearsed journey down her cheeks.

Yes, she *was* lucky. And as she watched two lumbering firemen carry out a table and some chairs, the astounding truth of it was so profound that she felt a slow smile soften the distressing lines of her face. The house was lovely and it was hers, but it didn't matter. It didn't give her security or love or happiness. Max and Dewey gave her that.

Max and Dewey—

His arms went around her from behind, capturing her. He pressed her back to him, kissing her hair, then turning her slowly to kiss her eye lids, to kiss away her tears.

"It's okay, Janie," he murmured softly. "It'll be okay."

"Max, you came..." She turned the rest of the way until she faced him completely. She pressed her head into his chest, and her tears soaked into the soft cotton of his shirt. "Max, how did you know?"

"That you love me? That there was a fire? That I can't go another hour without you?" He kissed her on the lips now, fully and deeply and without thought of fire or firemen or the smoke that blew around them.

Jane wrapped her arms around his neck. "Then...then you'll take me back?"

"You never left. Not really. Our love is strong. I was lonely there, miserable at times, but deep down I was okay."

Jane's voice was choked with tears. "Well I wasn't. All I knew was that I didn't have much left without you, Max. I need you so—"

"A two-way street, my love." He kissed away a tear that meandered down her cheek.

"I've been so foolish."

"Nope. You've had a lot to overcome. I think you've done an admirable job, darlin'."

"Because of you, Max. I finally saw it. Because of you I can do it. I think I can finally bury it all—"

"I think you can, too." Max held her in his arms and felt a joy so sweet he thought he ought to shout or sing or blow trumpets. Instead he buried his head in her hair and told her how much he loved her. "It's a forever sort of thing I'm after here, Janie."

"Forever sounds too short."

"We'll work on making it a long forever."

"I . . . I may still have some freaky moments, Max—"

"I think together Dewey and I can handle them. He called me from the farm tonight—"

"Dewey called you?"

Max nodded. "I got the call just as I walked in the door from a job in South Bend."

"Why?"

"He said he was spending the night out there and that you might be lonesome. He suggested I come over—"

"—and unlonesome me?"

"His exact words."

"And the fire? How did you know about the fire?"

"That I sensed. Or at least I sensed that something was wrong. Mrs. Atchity said a beautiful lady had come by and left a note. I couldn't find it and you didn't answer your phone. So I came right over. I talked to one of the firemen before I found you." *Because I was nearly frantic with fear. Because if I lost you, Jane, my life would be worth as much as those ashes on the kitchen floor. I couldn't go through that again. Not with you ...* But he didn't tell her that. Instead he held her and said softly, "The fireman said the damage isn't too bad. Mostly the kitchen."

Jane nodded against his chest. And then she took a deep breath and looked up into his eyes. "Well," she asked, "will you?"

"What?"

"Unlonesome me."

"Yeah, I might be able to fit it in."

"It might take a while. How long do you have?"

"A lifetime or two is all."

"I think maybe that will do it." Jane lifted her head to meet his kiss.

And with seven firemen and their exhausted hoses as witnesses, their lifetimes were sealed forever.

Epilogue

—

(Six years later...)

"You have reached the residence of Max and Jane Harris. Oh, yeah, and of me, Dewey and the other kids—Claire, Pete, Michael and Katy and baby Leo. We can't come to the phone right now because we're sailing on this cool boat to the Galapagos Islands with Uncle Leo. He says we can ride the turtles and watch the thirteen-year-old girls. Yea! We'll be home after we finish celebrating Uncle Leo's ninetieth birthday. But anyway, like leave a message at the beep because we'll get back to you sooner or later...." *Beep.*

* * * * *

COMING NEXT MONTH

#559 SUNSHINE—Jo Ann Algermissen
A Florida alligator farm? It was just what ad exec Rob Emery *didn't*
need! But sharing the place with Angelica Franklin made life with the
large lizards oh, so appealing....

#560 GUILTY SECRETS—Laura Leone
Leah McCargar sensed sexy houseguest Adam Jordan was not *all* he
claimed. But before she could prove him guilty of lying, she became
guilty... of love.

#561 THE HIDDEN PEARL—Celeste Hamilton
Aunt Eugenia's final match may be her toughest! Can Jonah
Pendleton coax shy Maggie O'Grady into leading a life of adventure?
The next book in the series *Aunt Eugenia's Treasures*.

#562 LADIES' MAN—Raye Morgan
Sensible Trish Becker knew that Mason Ames was nothing more than
a good-looking womanizer! But she still couldn't stop herself from
succumbing to his seductive charms.

#563 KING OF THE MOUNTAIN—Joyce Thies
Years ago Gloria Hubbard had learned that rough, tough William
McCann was one untamable man. Now he was back in town... and
back in her life.

#564 SCANDAL'S CHILD—Ann Major
When May's *Man of the Month* Officer Garret Cagan once again
saved scandalous Noelle Martin from trouble, the Louisiana bayou
wasn't the only thing steaming them up....

AVAILABLE NOW—

the books you've been waiting for by one of America's top romance authors!

DIANA PALMER

DUETS

Ten years ago Diana Palmer published her very first romances. Powerful and dramatic, these gripping tales of love are everything you have come to expect from Diana Palmer.

This month some of these titles are available again in **DIANA PALMER DUETS**—a special three-book collection. Each book has two wonderful stories plus an introduction by the author. You won't want to miss them!

Book 1
SWEET ENEMY
LOVE ON TRIAL

Book 2
STORM OVER THE LAKE
TO LOVE AND CHERISH

Book 3
IF WINTER COMES
NOW AND FOREVER

Available now at your favorite retail outlet.

 Silhouette Books®

You'll flip . . . your pages won't!
Read paperbacks *hands-free* with

Book Mate • I

The perfect "mate" for all your romance paperbacks

**Traveling • Vacationing • At Work • In Bed • Studying
• Cooking • Eating**

Perfect size for all standard paperbacks, this wonderful invention makes reading a pure pleasure! Ingenious design holds paperback books OPEN and FLAT so even wind can't ruffle pages — leaves your hands free to do other things. Reinforced, wipe-clean vinyl-covered holder flexes to let you turn pages without undoing the strap . . . supports paperbacks so well, they have the strength of hardcovers!

Pages turn WITHOUT opening the strap

SEE-THROUGH STRAP

Reinforced back stays flat

Built in bookmark

BOOK MARK

BACK COVER
HOLDING STRIP

10" x 7¼". opened.
Snaps closed for easy carrying. too

Available now. Send your name, address, and zip code, along with a check or money order for just $5.95 + .75¢ for postage & handling (for a total of $6.70) payable to Reader Service to:

Reader Service
Bookmate Offer
901 Fuhrmann Blvd.
P.O. Box 1396
Buffalo, N.Y. 14269-1396

Offer not available in Canada
*New York and Iowa residents add appropriate sales tax.

BM-G